SAY

MY

NAME

Also by Allegra Huston

Love Child: A Memoir of Family Lost and Found

SAY MY NAME

ALLEGRA HUSTON

ONE PLACE. MANY STORIES

HQ
An imprint of HarperCollins*Publishers* Ltd.
1 London Bridge Street
London SE1 9GF

This edition 2017

1

First published in Great Britain by
HQ, an imprint of HarperCollins*Publishers* Ltd. 2017

ISBN: HB: 978-0-00-820323-8
TPB: 978-0-00-820324-5

Printed and bound by
CPI Group (UK) Ltd, Croydon, CR0 4YY

For you, my battered angel

1

There, under a table heaped with china of the sort nobody uses anymore, she spots it, almost hidden behind random objects carrying price stickers faded by time. Daylight filters through grimy windows onto worn green velvet, golden wood. Strangely, the case is open—as if it's hoping to be found.

It's bigger than a violin, much smaller than a cello. It's fat, squarer than most instruments of its kind, with an elongated neck, and—this is what draws Eve in—encrusted with vines. The fragile carvings seem greener. They were once painted, maybe.

Eve moves the piles of junk aside so that she can crawl under the table. Usually she wears jeans for these expeditions, but it's a hot New York summer, so this morning she chose a thin dress, counting on the intricate print to disguise any smudges. It will rip easily, though, so she tucks up the sides into her underwear to keep it off the floor.

As she crouches down, the bones of her knees crack. Though she's fit and strong, her forty-eight-year-old body is starting to show age. Her brown hair has almost no gray in it—good genes, her mother would have said—but soon she'll have to decide whether to color it. She's never seen the point of lying about her age and, being married, she's less concerned about looking young than she might be if she were single. Still, the ugly milestone looms. She's tied her hair in a ponytail and covered her head with a scarf to protect against cobwebs.

By profession, Eve is a garden designer. Her husband, Larry, makes enough as a product development manager for a pill-coating supplier to pharmaceutical companies to enable him to treat her little business as, basically, a hobby. This annoys her, but the truth is, she treats it that way too. Taking it more seriously would mean confronting Larry and claiming ownership of her time and priorities, which she is not prepared to do. The status quo feels fragile, although it also feels as lasting as mortal life allows. All that's required is that she keep the delicate political balance, and doesn't rock the boat or disturb the sleeping dogs. She's gotten into the habit of not pushing any communication past the minimum required for practical matters and the appearance of enough closeness to assure her that their marriage is sound.

On weekends, guiltless and free, she searches out treasures for her friend Deborah's antique shop. Larry doesn't complain; she suspects he's glad to have the house to himself. For her part, she's glad to be away from it. The strange objects she finds ignite her imagination, conjuring up lives more exciting, and more terrifying, than the low-intensity safety of her own. Today she's exploring a northerly part of New

York City that, like a tidal pool left by successive immigrant waves, houses people from nations that may or may not still exist: Assyrians, Armenians, Macedonians, Baluchistanis. The alphabets in which the signs are written change block by block. Neighborhoods like this are her favorite hunting grounds.

On her hands and knees under the table, she tugs at the instrument in its case. It shifts with a jerk, leaving a hard outline of oily dust on the floor. Probably it hasn't been moved in years. She lifts it up onto a tin chest, keeping her back to the storekeeper to disguise her interest.

The vines twine over the body of the instrument and up its neck, stretching out into the air. Though the delicacy of the carving is almost elfin, it has the strength of vines: blindly reaching, defying gravity. The tendrils are dotted with small flowers: jasmine, so accurately rendered that Eve identifies them instantly. A flap of velvet in the lid conceals a bow, held in place by ribbons. It, too, is twined with curling vines.

She wiggles her fingers into the gaps between the instrument and the velvet lining, prying it loose. A moth flies out into her face and disappears in the slanting shafts of light.

Holding it by the neck, she senses another shape. With spit and the hem of her dress, she cleans away the dust. There's a pudgy, babyish face, the vines tightening their weave across its eyes. Cupid, blinded by love.

Eve pinches up dust from the floor to dirty the face again. She has learned not to improve the appearance of things until after the bargaining is done and the money has changed hands. Then she turns the instrument over.

The back is in splinters.

Eve touches her finger to the ragged shards of wood, longing to make this beautiful thing whole again. The damage must have been deliberate: an accident would have broken off the vines. What drove that person over the brink? Musician's frustration? Rage at fate? Heartbreak? She can almost feel remnants of the emotion stuck to the gash, like specks of dried blood.

If she had it repaired, the cost would almost certainly be more than the instrument is worth. And even an expert might not be able to restore it completely. It could serve as a decorative item, but only if the gash stays hidden. Deborah won't want it—she has a rule against broken things. Also, she feels more comfortable with things that have names, like bowls and vases and candlesticks. Passionless things that sit prettily in nice rooms. The history that this object bears on its back would freak her out.

Eve moves to return the instrument to its exile, but she can't bring herself to do it. Now that she has touched it, she cannot push it back into the shadows.

It's an extravagance, driving into Manhattan: the cost of parking; the idling crosstown traffic. But Eve needed her car for her expedition to the outer boroughs, and she is not ready to go home to New Jersey. She finds an expensive space in an elevator lot, and starts walking the eight blocks to the Public Library. She leaves the strange instrument, in its case, on the back seat beside a curly wrought-iron birdcage she picked up earlier.

"Eve? Eve Armanton?"

She looks around, unsure where this urgent voice is coming from. She has barely heard her maiden name since college.

"Eve! I can't believe it!"

"Robert?"

Robert Burnett, her brother Bill's best friend. And, beside him, a younger man who must be his son. The pair of them hit her like an optical illusion, a thirty-year warp in time: Robert now and Robert then, standing side by side on 34th Street. The son is, Eve realizes, even more beautiful than his father used to be, with thick black hair, a finely cut nose, and angled eyebrows over long, wide-set eyes. Age has dragged Robert's once-fine jawline into jowls, and thinned his hair. The bright blue eyes that enthralled her when she was fifteen are murky, and there's a sheen to his skin as if the cholesterol in his bloodstream is seeping through.

Back then, Robert reminded her of Tigger, with his bouncing energy and his recklessness. He and Bill were twenty-two: college roommates, party boys, the world at their feet. Everything seemed to come easily to Robert—but Bill saw shadows where Robert saw only the light. Robert's wildness was pure exuberance; Bill, Eve sensed with a teenager's unspeakable anxiety, was daring fate, as if hurrying up the tragedy he knew would surely come. Eve has barely thought of Robert since her brother's funeral. After Bill's death, she cut off all connection with the elements of his life, terrified that the darkness that drove him to suicide might invade her too.

Robert moves more slowly now, his boisterousness reined in by years of office-bred decorum, the crazy Hawaiian shirts he used to wear replaced by a well-cut suit, pink shirt, and brightly patterned tie. She knows what he wants to do, and she will let him do it, for old times' sake: sweep her up in a hug and spin her round and round until they both get dizzy. Bill used to do that when he saw Eve after a gap of weeks, and the fact that Bill did it became Robert's permission, a fond mastery over his friend's little sister, whose adoration he accepted, without comment or attention, as his due.

Robert's arms lifting her feel as strong as they always did. Cars, pedestrians, storefronts whirl past in a circular blur. Eve scrambles for a reference point, as she was taught in childhood ballet class, and there it is, like a hook catching her searching eyes: the younger man's gaze, his eyes a startling green, strobing as Robert whirls her around.

Finally, she feels concrete under her feet again. Robert keeps hold of her arm to prevent them both from falling. Bill used to love it when she fell over: a big brother's affectionate cruelty.

"How long has it been?" Robert's face is alight with the pleasure of finding her.

"Twenty-nine years. Almost."

"The funeral."

Eve nods. It took place in November. Leaves stripped from the trees, naked branches that made her think of her brother's dead bones.

"You remember, we had a baby with us? Well, here he is. Mick, meet Eve."

"Micajah," he says, gently correcting his father. A name she's never heard before. *Mic-KAY-jah*. She likes the roll of it.

He holds out his hand. "Eve," he says.

She's reluctant to touch him, as if she might be touching an electrified fence. As his fingers close around her hand, her nerves register the calluses on his fingertips. She drops her eyes. He's wearing jeans and a loose blue shirt, the sleeves partly rolled. His feet, in hiker's flip-flops, are sinewy, with long toes. She feels suddenly that she shouldn't be looking at them, these body parts naked to her gaze.

"Eve's brother taught me everything I know about music," says Robert. "Which, granted, compared to you, Mick, isn't all that much. My son, I want you to know, Eve, is a rock star."

"I play in a band." His voice is low, almost hoarse—nothing like Robert's. His words are no more than an explanation to tone down his father's boast.

"Inked the last clauses of the deal this morning." Robert

pats his son's shoulder. "We're celebrating with lunch. Join us, Eve! Whoever you're meeting, stand him up!"

This is the Robert she knew: someone who embraced the world with such total disregard for the possibility of rejection that it couldn't resist him. He was always on to the next thing, always excited, as forceful as a tornado. It fascinated and frightened her, the way the past just fell away behind him into a detritus of facts stripped of meaning. She used to wonder whether anything could really be precious to him.

In memory of Bill, Eve says yes to lunch.

"It's an old Shaker name," Micajah tells Eve as they walk, in response to her question. "My great-great-great-great-grandfather's brother was an architect, the first Micajah Burnett. The first I know of, anyway."

"I visited a Shakertown in Kentucky once," she says, "when I was driving my son to college. It was one of the most beautiful places I've ever been."

She remembers the elegant symmetry: twin staircases, twinned rooms, to keep the men and the women apart. And the sense of tranquility, which she imagined had always reigned there, since there were no marriages, no children, no sex.

Micajah has his father's excellent manners; but, where Robert held chairs and doors the way a peacock holds his splayed tail, Micajah holds Eve's chair for her in an offhand way, as if in casual rebellion against the carelessness of the world. Eve never agreed with the militant college feminists that such manners were insulting; she taught her own son to hold doors, though not just for women. Once she stood outside the door of the bank for several minutes as people went in and out, waiting for the eight-year-old Allan to realize she hadn't followed his heedless rush toward the M&M dispenser inside.

"Looks like you were scrubbing floors this morning."

She noticed Micajah registering the grubby hem of her dress and the smudges on her knees as she sat down. She'd tried to wipe them clean in the car, but the dirt had ground itself into her skin.

"I was dragging something out from under a table, in a junk shop in the Bronx. I was on my way to the library to research it when your father waylaid me."

"That's cool," he says. "That you don't care your knees are dirty." The corners of his mouth turn down when he smiles, as if he's keeping back some of his amusement for himself. "What was it?"

"A musical instrument. I don't know what you'd call it. I've never seen anything like it before." Eve isn't sure if he's teasing her. Luckily, the instrument makes a convenient conversational shield. "It's like a violin—strings and a bow—but squarer, with a really long neck."

"Sounds like the kind of thing Mick plays," says Robert. "Weird contraptions that don't even have English names."

There's a sudden edge in his voice: annoyance, or jealousy? Praising Micajah, he was feeding his own ego, Eve realizes, and she dislikes being his audience: for the showing off and the putting down. She's starting to wish, for more than one reason, that she hadn't agreed to join them for lunch.

"My dad thinks I'm a terrorist," Micajah says, unruffled. "Because I play music from places where the State Department doesn't want you to go."

His vibe is somewhere between bohemian and outlaw.

"Well, if it makes you millions, I won't complain!" Robert's laugh is a braying bark. Eve sees the couple at the nearest table stiffen and pretend to ignore him.

"Yeah, all that money," says Micajah quietly. "I'm planning to spend it on gold-leaf underwear. Not ostentatious. Just for that coddled feeling."

The corners of his mouth turn down. His eyes, mischievous, catch Eve's. She feels a trickle of sweat run down her back, even though it's cool inside the restaurant. The sports bra she chose for her hunting expedition feels like an implement of torture around her chest.

"You're going to move out of that roach motel," Robert says. "Buy something that's going to appreciate."

"I appreciate where I live now," says Micajah. Then, to Eve: "Did you buy it?"

"Yes."

"You're a musician?"

"No. But even if I was, it's not playable. The back is smashed."

"So why did you buy it?"

"It's beautiful," she says.

"And you couldn't just leave it there."

She feels transparent to his eyes.

"If it wasn't broken, I probably couldn't have afforded it," she says. "It has this incredible carving, vines, twining all over it. I'm pretty sure it's jasmine. It made me think of the secret gardens in children's books. Or *The Arabian Nights*."

"How the hell do you know it's jasmine? It's wood, for Chrissake." That's the spoiled-brat side of Robert: hating not being the center of Eve's attention.

She reaches into her purse for a business card, and gives it to him. "I'm a garden designer now. I use jasmine a lot. It's resilient, it lasts all summer, and it smells delicious when you sit outside in the evenings."

Robert holds the card at arm's length, as if he doesn't believe what's written on it. Eve had no particular interest in flowers back when he knew her. She gets the sense that he considers her change over the years as a kind of betrayal.

Micajah is glancing from his father to Eve, clearly wondering if they were once lovers. They weren't. Eve is a little shocked by how much she cares that Micajah should know that. As the little sister, she had a DON'T TOUCH sign plastered to her forehead. When Bill died, she went to the funeral with the guilty thought that maybe the extremity of emotion might propel them into each other's arms. She hated herself for this callous disloyalty to her brother, allowing her desire to contaminate what should have been the purity of her grief.

She didn't know, before she got to the church, that Robert was married with a baby son.

The waiter arrives, a plate in each hand and the third balanced on his wrist. He gives Robert his steak, Eve her salad. Conscientiously, she ordered from the cheaper end of the menu.

"Saltimbocca," the waiter says, setting Micajah's plate on the table, twisting it to its most advantageous angle. "Jumps into the mouth. That's what it means." He's flirting, helpless as an iron filing in Micajah's magnetic field. Earlier, when he took their orders, Eve registered his agitation. She feels a pang of sympathy for him. Women used to be like that around Robert. She'd seen girls chase him down the street and force their phone numbers on him. He gloried in it with the laziness of a lion.

"Thanks, Josh," Micajah says, remembering the waiter's name from his spiel earlier, and meeting his eyes for a short moment before turning his attention back to Eve. Elegantly done, she thinks—a masculine gentleness his father never had.

"At least it's not roses," Micajah says.

What if the carved flowers had been roses? Would she have bought it? Maybe not. It was the jasmine—secretive, blooming in darkness—that seduced her.

"I hate roses," he adds.

"Why?"

"Drag queens of the flower world."

"Meaning what exactly?" his father chimes in. He looks from Eve to Micajah, Micajah to Eve, like a boxing referee before saying the word "Fight."

"The whole sickening cultural orthodoxy of them," Micajah says. "The fake valuation, like that 'a diamond is forever' crap. The environmental destruction of the factory rose farms, gobbling up the land in places like Kenya while the local people starve. It's like their whole purpose in the world is to lie. I screwed around on you, darling, so here's a bunch of roses. And that's not even getting into the S&M of it. A symbol of love that makes your fingers bleed? Except, no, let's pretend roses don't have thorns, and hire slum kids to slice them off with razors."

"He's a hothead," says Robert.

"I care," says Micajah. It seems like an old battle between them.

"Do you really think it's possible to have love without hurt?" Eve asks Micajah, then wishes she hadn't.

"I don't know," says Micajah. "Is it possible to love deeply and choose not to feel the pain? Hell, it's worth a try. Because if you don't, what happens? You end up wrecking what's beautiful."

Like Bill. And like that unknown person who smashed the instrument but couldn't bring himself to destroy it completely.

"Are you going to get it fixed?" Micajah asks Eve. "Or, you like broken things."

It's a statement, not a question. Again, she feels him looking straight into her heart. Flustered, she glances around the restaurant: the other diners chatting and laughing, the waiters moving competently about, the gerberas in vases on the tables.

"What were you doing in a junk shop in the Bronx, anyway?" asks Robert. "Looking for secondhand plants? I guess you found one!" That barking laugh again.

"Scouting for a friend's antique shop. It's what I do on weekends, sometimes. Now that my son's grown. Allan." Even after twenty-four years, she feels a warmth in saying his name. "He's in Cambodia right now, taking a year off after pre-med, working for Smile Train."

"What's that?" asks Robert, though he doesn't sound genuinely interested.

"A charity that fixes cleft palates on kids," says Micajah. "That's seriously cool," he says to Eve. "You're proud of him."

"I am."

"You should be proud of yourself too. You brought him up right."

Flustered, she manages a half-smile in response. She's glad she doesn't know what to say, as she doesn't trust her voice. Whatever words she'd find might come out as a squeak, or shaky, or have no sound at all.

"I'd never think you could have a grown son, if I didn't know better," says Robert with automatic chivalry.

Eve feels a warm, gentle pressure against her foot. As

she looks to Micajah in surprise, the pressure vanishes. Imperceptibly, he shakes his head.

No, what? Eve wonders. No, don't respond to him? No, you don't look younger than your age? No, you do—or you don't—but it doesn't matter?

Eve takes a drink of water and smells muskiness on her skin. There's a melting sensation at her core: her body is rushing ahead on a path she knows she should not follow. This boy—he's a boy, she insists to herself, though she knows he must be twenty-eight or twenty-nine—is throwing her off her axis. In college, she lived for that feeling. Before today, she thought she'd outgrown it, and comforted herself in the dull succession of her days with the relief of knowing she would never feel that fizzing confusion again.

When she dares to look back at Micajah, the green gaze is like a wave rushing across the space between them to drench her, sweep her up, carry her away. Stop! she thinks. But she does not want it to end.

2

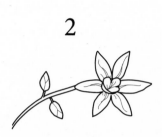

In the library, Eve forces herself to concentrate. The closest match she can find is called a viola d'amore, with a blindfolded cherub crowning its curving tip. But there is no other carving except the usual violin holes, and the blindfold is just a cloth. Plus, the shape of the viola d'amore's body is different, and it has many more strings. She cannot find anything like those eerily lifelike vines.

As she drives home, Micajah's words swirl around in Eve's head. Has he ever felt that depth of love and loss? she wonders. She would like to know.

This is wrong, she says to herself. Then she overlays the first judgment with another one: that she is being old-fashioned and anti-feminist. Yes, she is married; but that doesn't mean she should be caged and chaperoned like a Saudi wife. She is allowed to have male friends.

Still, the likelihood is that she will never see him again.

She makes an extra effort with dinner, buying halibut despite the expense. It was always Larry's favorite, but they haven't had it in the last year or so, since the day he came home from what he said was a company retreat and informed her that he'd found his totem animal. An "empowerment teacher" had led him on a vision quest, during which a wolf had appeared to him. The wolf, the guru told him, had come to guide him into the full expression of his self.

It was hard to imagine anyone less wolflike than Larry, but perhaps that was the point: the wolf's qualities were what he needed. She could see that. A vague dissatisfaction had been gnawing at him. He'd followed the signposted corporate path to a solid management job, but a bitterness had crept into his accounts of the office, and she realized that his success felt so bloodless to him, so mediocre, that it was beginning to feel more like defeat. He began to buy uncharacteristic articles of clothing—pink socks, a leather bomber jacket—which disappeared after a few outings.

"I feel like I'm an illusion of myself," he said to Eve once, in a rare moment of vulnerability. When she asked him what he meant, he couldn't quite explain: he was blurred into a mass of people, and the idea that he, Larry, was an individual person, distinct in any way, was just a trick. It wasn't a *Matrix*-like sci-fi horror vision; it didn't apply to everybody. Just him, and people like him. He was losing his outline, or doubting if he had ever had any, seeping into a general sludge.

From the first hours they spent together, Eve had loved Larry's surreal sense of humor, the way he imbued inanimate objects with motives and desires. It added a liveliness to his practical reliability. But he rarely found anything funny anymore. Eve felt a chill as she recognized, in that vision of human sludge, the imagination she'd once delighted in soured by despair.

He watched sports on TV as he always did, but his eyes became foggy, his hand held the beer bottle as awkwardly as an amateur actor holding a prop. He stopped seeing his old friends, and Eve doesn't know if he's made new ones. Their social life contracted, until Eve felt she could count her own friends on the fingers of one hand. Gradually, Larry moved into the spare bedroom: first his clothes, then his comb and nail clippers, and finally his nighttime self. The solidity, the sense of rational, practical certainty, that she was so strongly drawn to had abandoned him.

She has tried again and again to locate the moment in time when the slide started. But she cannot pin it down. His dissolution is like a creeping stain, reaching further and further into the past.

At first Eve welcomed Larry's inner wolf, as she would have welcomed anything that promised to help him find his sense of himself again. Now she hates it and distrusts it. Once he was gentle and considerate; now he has become brusque, even deliberately rude, and proud of himself for every selfish action and bad-tempered snap at the world. When Allan was little, he used to beg Eve to read *The Jungle Book* to him over and over again; she remembers those wolves as dignified, protective, family-oriented. Larry's feral inner self is a loner stalking through a kill-or-be-killed world. If only he'd read *The Jungle Book*, she thought.

Still, Larry was a good father. She loved to watch through the window as her menfolk played catch in the backyard, Larry contorting his body into bizarre shapes, Allan squealing with delight and trying to copy him. When Allan was a teenager, Larry took him on weekend fishing trips. Eve would ask what they did and Allan would always reply, "Nothing much." But she saw what that undemanding companionship did for Allan: gave him a quiet confidence, an even keel.

"My default setting is happy," Allan had reassured her when he opened his fifth rejection letter from medical school. She felt panicky, but he remained serenely sure that all would work out for the best. And it did.

The halibut is Eve's attempt to remind Larry of their sweet days, before every dinner had to consist of red meat. But when she calls him to the table, he doesn't come down for another ten minutes. By then the fish is dry and he eats it with an air of forbearance, as if he's taking one for the team. He picks up an asparagus spear, watches it droop, and drops it back on his plate with distaste. It's not my fault, Eve wants to scream at him, you're the one who spoiled dinner.

"I'm sorry. It cooked too long," she says, but then adds, "during the time before you came downstairs."

"You could have given me some warning," he says. "I was in the middle of something important."

"Something for work?" she asks, hoping to jump-start the conversation.

"No."

The instrument, hidden inside its case, sits on the sideboard behind Larry. Eve has prepared her tale of sleuthing through the flotsam of displaced nations and has been looking forward to telling it. Larry rarely asks about her day, and recently he has been sharing little of his own, so Eve has fallen into the habit of rehearsing their dinner-table conversation while she cooks. Now, however, she's unwilling to offer up the instrument on the altar of forced companionship. If she did, she'd be exposing it to another blow—from Larry's self-absorbed indifference. She feels an urge to protect it, like a lost child that she's taken charge of until its mother is found.

"I'm going for a run," he says, standing up before swallowing his last mouthful. He's lost weight in the past year, and looks lean and slim. The fact that he's healthier is the very thin silver lining.

He folds his napkin, drops a kiss on her cheek, and reaches into a cupboard for a stick of beef jerky on the way out. A year ago, he would have helped her clear up.

As she lies in bed that night, Eve realizes that not once during the lunch with Robert and Micajah did she mention her husband. She deliberately mentioned Allan, and she mentioned her business, wanting Robert and Micajah to see her as an independent woman and not just somebody's wife. But does that mean she had to behave as if she was nobody's wife? She wonders why neither of them asked—especially since she was wearing a wedding ring.

Half of that question is easy to answer. Robert didn't care. He was delighted to see her only because she would be a mirror to reflect back to him his own glory as a father and a lawyer both. Any old or new acquaintance would have served.

And the other half?

Micajah didn't care either. Which can have different meanings. One of which could be that, like her, he didn't want to bring a husband into the space between them.

She tries to trace it back, to the first moment when she felt the beam of Micajah's focus locking onto her. Before he brushed against her foot; before the talk of roses. When she caught him eying her dirty knees? No: out on the sidewalk when Robert whirled her round. It was she who sought his eyes, to stabilize herself. By the time she was standing on firm ground again, the connection was made.

Then, later, that shockingly intimate gaze. Could such a look have existed across the distance of a restaurant table? It was, she imagines now, how he would look at her if they were making love. It said, We are so joined, so complete, that the rest of the world does not exist. Meeting it was like riding a rodeo horse. When Micajah turned to his father and said something teasing, that was the eight-second buzzer. Whatever he said, whatever Robert replied, was white noise in her ears. That's when she reached for her handbag, made an excuse about a just-remembered appointment, and left.

She has never seen that look in Larry's eyes. He looked at her with love in their early years, a sparkle of pleasure at a quirk of speech or an idiosyncratic movement. But sex had always been basically a roll-on, roll-off deal. She'd thought that was how he wanted it. He'd glance at her quickly and look away, as if he was embarrassed or didn't want to force her to look at him. Now she wonders if he didn't dare to pause and pour his heart into hers, for fear she would close hers against him.

I might have, Eve realizes with a lurch. I was scared too.

It was the same fear that Larry felt: fear of being fully seen. She and Larry both wanted to be what the other wanted them to be; they hid their frailties, were ashamed of their faults. Maybe, she thinks, he thought that I loved an idea of him—a partial person, not the whole. He dreaded being seen—and so did I.

Now, after being held in the beam of Micajah's steady gaze, she yearns for it. The very unlikeliness of his interest in her made pretense absurd.

Did she ever really, truly love Larry? Even yesterday, she would have answered yes, she did. Now, lying in bed, thinking about Micajah, the truth is that she doesn't know.

I am being ridiculous, she tells herself, panicking. He

touched my foot by accident. He probably looks at everyone that way. There's no reason he would be interested in me.

Maybe he has a mother complex, she thinks. But that comes as a comfort, not a diagnosis—a possibility, not a problem. It wouldn't be enough to make her say no.

And there she is, back again, like a compass needle dragged inescapably to the north.

The next day, Eve wakes with the spider on her face. It's been there most mornings, for months now—a heavy darkness pressing on her brow, reaching sharp points into her eyes, her sinuses, cracking the corners of her mouth, making her head ache from the bones out.

Her breathing is shallow, though she's so used to it that she hardly notices. Her stomach feels sour, as it usually does until she brushes her teeth. Her thighs are lead weights, and her feet are hot and uncomfortable. She sleeps with them outside the covers and often they're cold, but there's no way to warm them without the raging heat. Sometimes she fantasizes about chopping them off.

Many mornings, she rolls over and buries her face in the pillow, longing to drop back into unconsciousness. When that fails, she lies prone, one arm across her eyes, summoning the strength of will to greet the new day with optimism—what her mother used to call a good disposition. Eve dislikes people who feel sorry for themselves. She deals with her own burden of darkness by leaving it in her bed and, once upright, pretending firmly that it isn't there.

Her heart thuds, too hard and too fast, as if it is trying to rev up the momentum to run away. It will calm down soon, as it always does; the thought of coffee helps. A latte, warm and bittersweet, soothes the jagged edges of her nerves. She will walk to the coffee shop and have somebody make one for her. She allows herself this luxury a couple of times a week, on days when she needs to feel cared for.

She resolves that today she will put all thoughts of Micajah from her mind. The name draws her back to that Shakertown and its naive, decorous purity. Since sex was forbidden, the sect grew only by conversion. No wonder it died out.

She hears Larry in the hallway, his door opening then shutting. They too sleep separately, but in resentful, repressed inequality rather than in equable, asexual peace. The bathroom Larry uses is not en suite; it also serves the room that Eve still thinks of as Allan's. Though he keeps his bedroom door closed unless he's actually walking through it, he leaves the bathroom door open. It's a territorial power play that Eve accepts as a quid pro quo for his acceptance of the lower-status bedroom. She won't go into the hallway until she hears his footsteps on the stairs.

The rasp of the blender drifts up from the kitchen. Larry is making his morning smoothie. Its ingredients are kept in a special drawer in the fridge into which nothing else is allowed, and which he has requested her not to open. Maybe he's putting raw meat in it, she thinks, but the joke—if it is a joke—isn't funny.

She's hungry. Her stomach is clenching. Feeling treasonous for not wanting to see him or talk to him, she waits for the businesslike bang of the door. Then she will get up and revel in the empty house. He's going to Arizona for work this week, and she's looking forward to a few days of solitude.

Things are easier now that he has his own room. In the last years when they shared a bed, they would wake and turn away from each other if they weren't turned away already. They would exchange cursory good mornings and she would ask, "What do you want for breakfast?" and dutifully she would have cereal, or eggs, or French toast, waiting for him when he came downstairs. The secret smoothies are a blessing too. Until she stopped doing it, she had no idea how much she resented starting her day by serving him.

She asked her son the same question, every day until he left home. She mulls it over as she lies in bed: how she has perpetuated the servitude by training the next generation to expect it. But isn't that what a good mother does? When her mother said it to her, it was different: training by example, the flip side. She got breakfast for her father and her brother on the days when her mother lingered in bed.

Until the moment he left her, Eve's mother served Eve's father. She brought him a drink when he came home from work, she asked solicitously about his day, she never questioned that he did nothing to help with the cooking or the cleaning up, when she had had a far more stressful day with five children to care for than he could have had, in his well-appointed office with a well-appointed secretary. The details have changed, not the dynamics. The serving has become subtler: buying Christmas presents for Larry's mother, praising him for taking any small share of the housework, making "Daddy time" the family priority. As the years tick by, Eve is starting to understand why in more brutal days old women were reviled, exiled, burned as witches: they'd stopped worshipping at the shrine. They could see that it was all just smoke and mirrors.

As Eve sits at the kitchen table, eating a slice of the apricot tart she made for dessert last night but didn't serve, her phone pings. She gets few texts now that Allan is out of the country. Mostly they're from Deborah. But this is too early for Deborah. She doesn't open her store until noon so she can lie in bed late.

"Mornings are the best," she said lasciviously once, enjoying Eve's discomfort. "I get to spend time with my little friend. Actually, a really nice big friend! Poor Ted, he never measured up, but then what man does? No man around here, anyway. Once you go wired, you never get tired. You should try it, Eve. Stop being such a born-again virgin!" Deborah knows about Larry's move into the guest room.

Eve has thought about it in a desultory way, but the idea of going to a sex shop is repellent. She's afraid that if she searches online, ads for sex toys and hookup sites will haunt her screen forever. At times, she has wondered if she has any libido left. Menopause hasn't really started to show yet, but maybe loss of interest in sex was the first sign.

The text is from a number she doesn't recognize, with an area code she doesn't recognize.

Hi, Eve. Send me a photo maybe I can help. M
Micajah.

For a crazy moment, her imagination spirals into naked selfies, compromised celebrities and politicians. She laughs out loud at herself. The tumultuous return of her libido, yesterday, is disturbing and intoxicating. She's tired of feeling guilty over Larry. For now, she will put her guilt aside.

Micajah is simply offering to help. Or rather, it *would* be simple, if not for that "M".

She knows she doesn't actually need help. The instrument was an impulse buy, and she can easily absorb the sixty dollars it cost. She can stash it away and forget it. Allan can throw it in the garbage when she's dead.

She goes to the dining room and opens the case. The choice is plain: save it or send it to its grave. Strange, how this inanimate object has the quality of a living creature. She picks it up with both hands and turns it over, where the splintered wood is pale and raw against the golden varnish that, in this clear light, has the mottled depth of centuries.

She cannot trash this; it's impossible. She wants the wound mended.

She sets it on the table where the light shows it best and snaps four photos: a wide shot, close-ups of the carved vines and the leaf-blinded Cupid, and the horrible gash in the back. As she waits for the *whoosh* that tells her the last text has gone, she fits the instrument back into its case. The vines seem to be reaching toward her, to pull her in, to twine her together with Micajah.

He phones twenty minutes later. She feels her heart pound as the number lights up her phone. She lets it ring, willing herself to calm down, but any longer and it will go to voicemail, so she swipes her finger quickly across the screen.

"I think I can help," he says.

"You know someone who could fix it?"

"Yes."

"Can you give me his number?"

"I don't know if it's a good idea."

"Why not?"

"He's . . . tricky."

"Oh," she says.

She feels like a stammering teenager, and hopes he can't tell. She used to love to picture the physical connection between herself and Larry as they talked: the receiver held against her ear, the spiraling cord linking it to the phone, then the wires and cables threading through the miles to where Larry was, another spiraling cord, and the receiver touching his ear.

But the electrons whizzing between her and Micajah leave no trace. She imagines an airy chain of particles and waves, with millions and billions of other chains whizzing through it, as insubstantial as magic.

"Meet me," he says.

She's on the verge of saying, Can't you just give me his number? Instead, she says, "When?"

They settle on the following Thursday. He gives her an address.

Micajah's persistence makes Eve feel special in a way she never has before. Larry's judgment didn't carry the authority of Micajah's, even though Micajah is essentially a stranger. She was special to Larry when they were young, but she knew that didn't make her objectively special. There was nothing extraordinary about her; it was just that she was a good fit for him. He was not extraordinary either, which appealed to her then. She suspected she had a streak of Bill's wildness in her—she was drawn to stories of adventure, rebellious thoughts that she let loose into the air like helium balloons. When it killed him, she determined to kill it in herself.

For five days, she is walking on eggshells. She is certain that Micajah does not feel the same.

3

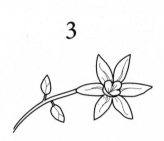

The club has no sign. It's on the Upper East Side, a quiet part of Manhattan. The streets feature well-groomed older women walking very well-groomed small dogs, and occasional uniformed nannies pushing strollers built like mountain bikes. It is the middle of the day, so there are no visible men.

Two chic, beautiful girls sit behind an ornate desk.

"I'm meeting Micajah Burnett."

"Ms. Armanton?"

"Yes." It feels transgressive, admitting to her maiden name.

"He's waiting for you in the library."

The second girl presses a button. Eve hears a discreet buzz. A doorman opens an inner door. Eve has never been in a place like this: oozing comfort, patinated with money, every surface polished or faux-painted or plushly cushioned.

She spots Micajah in a corner, beneath the oak paneling, the glow of a lamp reflecting off his dark hair. He's sitting in an armchair. A backgammon board lies open on a low table. He rises when he sees her.

"You came."

"You thought I wouldn't?"

"I figured maybe you said yes just to get me off the phone. You're too polite to hang up on me."

"And too polite not to turn up when I said I would, I guess."

Her smile moves quickly beyond politeness, as if Micajah has lassoed it and pulled it close to him.

"What is this place? It's quite something."

"A club. Favored by older British rock stars, South American drug lords with surgically altered faces, and Russian oligarchs."

"And you?"

"On special occasions."

His clothes are scruffy in the way of movie stars caught by paparazzi in the park: jeans, T-shirt, creased cotton jacket. Flip-flops, as on the day they first met. Smooth, square toe-nails.

"Two sisters," he says, following her eyeline. "You get used to getting pedicures."

She can't tell if he's joking or not. To cover, she focuses on the backgammon board, the pieces set up ready to play on their eight sharp points. It is made of chocolate-colored leather, with points of alternating cream and ocher outlined in gold tooling. The pieces are discs of agate and white marble. It is a board for emperors and plutocrats. She runs her finger along a seam where two colors of leather meet, inset-sewn rather than appliquéd so that there is no obstruction to the pieces sliding across them.

"Dad told me you're pretty good."

"I was," she says. "I haven't played since my brother died."

"That must have been tough for you. My dad . . ." He shrugs. We're different from him, the silence says. No need to say more.

"I ordered tea," he says, sitting down.

"Tea's perfect." People who have assignations do not drink tea. It is possible, and acceptable, to drink tea with the offspring of one's friends.

He gives her a piece of paper with a name and phone number on it. "This is the luthier I know," he says. "The man who'd be able to fix your instrument. His name is Yann Logue. He's eccentric. Don't be put off by his manner, he's not trying to be rude. It's not personal."

"I thought you didn't want me to call him," Eve says.

"The best way would be if we just took it to him," says Micajah. "But you've got his number, in case you never want to see me again."

She stashes it in her handbag, after a glance to make sure she can read his writing. It's almost calligraphic, each letter formed with care. She wonders if he always writes like that.

"Sorry if I offended you the other day," he says as he pours from a teapot perched on a side table. "Maybe you love roses."

"I like climbing roses. But lots of people want formal rose gardens."

"Status symbol?"

"I suppose. Or just lack of imagination." She takes a sip of tea. "Did you know there's a rose called Richard M. Nixon?"

"With the M?"

"Yes."

"That's actually revolting."

He reaches behind his chair and brings out a bunch of spectacular, full-blown peonies, a wet paper towel wrapped around their stems.

"I don't know if they'll last long enough for you to get them home."

"They're far more beautiful than roses."

A young man— Waiter? Bellboy? Concierge-in-training?— materializes with a vase half full of water. He places it on the side table and departs.

"Did you arrange that?" she asks Micajah.

"They're good here. They think of everything."

"You did." He escapes the accusation rather than denying it, by picking up his dice cup and raising it toward her as if he's making a toast.

"Shall we play?"

"Sure." She picks up her own cup. He tips one die into his palm and rolls the other. A six. She does the same. A six also. She feels a twinge of embarrassment, as if she's done it intentionally to flirt with him.

"Game on," he says, turning the doubling cube to two.

The game comes back to her. She finds herself able to move her pieces without counting, to know instinctively when to risk getting hit and when to close ranks and protect. It's a relief not to have to talk. She lets the rhythm of the game take her, the ebb and flow of the energy across the board, his hand reaching toward her when he moves his pieces and withdrawing as he collects his dice, her hand reaching toward him when it's her turn. She finds herself staring at his long fingers as they slide the marble discs into place.

"Double you."

He pushes the cube toward her. She looks into his eyes, green flecked with gold. She does not need to look at the board to know that she will say yes. After all, there's nothing at stake.

She takes the cube with her left hand, and notices the glint of her wedding ring.

They play for nearly two hours. The board belongs to the hotel, he tells her; it's why he invited her here. She asks about his band, and he tells her that their name is Blisskrieg, though they may change it to Metropolis because the label thinks Blisskrieg looks weird in print. They've been together for nine years, he says. It's been a long road to what's shaping up to be their overnight success. She's pleased she can see, even in this softly lit room, the beginnings of lines around his eyes.

"What instrument do you play?" she asks.

"Lots of them. Fiddle mostly, and cello. Whatever gives the track an edge. Accordion sometimes. I just started learning theremin."

"What's a theremin? I've never heard of it."

"A man named Léon Theremin invented it. It sounds like a zombie opera singer and it looks like something out of Dr. Frankenstein's laboratory. You play it without touching it. It picks up the electrical energy from your hands."

"So it's like you're playing the air?"

"Exactly!" He's excited that she's understood so quickly. She is too.

"I'd love to see that," she says.

"I'll show you," he says. "Next time."

So there will be a next time. It's agreed.

She wins an eight-point game and he gives her a high-five. It feels like a stopping place. By tacit agreement, they don't reset the pieces. He checks the time on his phone.

"Teatime's over," he says. "It's cocktail hour."

"I should be getting home," she says. Though Larry is not due back from his business trip until tomorrow, and the cat can look after itself.

"Just one?"

He stands, and holds out his hand to her.

"Not here?"

"Kind of," he says. "And kind of not."

Again, that feeling of the horse under her—not bucking, but picking up speed. Yes, she should be going home, back to the safety of her home and the sanctity of her marriage vows. But there are reins this time; she can control it.

"All right," she says. "One."

He grabs a backpack from the floor and, after checking

that nobody is watching, leads her to an unobtrusive door for staff only, ushering her through into a tiny space with another door blocking the way. He digs in a pocket, fishes out an ID card on a lanyard, and slides it through the reader.

"You work here?" Eve asks, happy that this extravagant venue now makes some kind of sense.

"Art deliveries," he explains in a low voice, almost a whisper. "People actually live here. The kind of people who don't want visitors to come inside their apartment, and don't want to go outside. Too famous. Too wanted, in every sense of the word. They buy art, of course. Very expensive, large art, which somebody has to deliver. Which would be me."

"So we're sneaking in?"

Eve is the kind of person whose heart races when she sees a cop car, even if she isn't speeding.

"Does it bother you?"

The thought of getting caught does, but she left caution behind when she left her house hours ago, and adrenaline is fueling her now. She feels like a kid sneaking into her parents' bedroom when they're out for the evening. She will discover something forbidden. She will learn secrets.

Micajah conducts her quickly through the service passageways to an elevator, and presses the button for the highest floor. Once the doors close, he speaks in a normal voice. "This"— he gestures with the ID card, —"is because I got a temp pass one time. Complicated installation piece, lots of in and out. The night shift was on duty when I left and they forgot to ask for it back. So later, I took it to this guy I know."

"What kind of guy?"

"The kind of guy who can turn a day card into an all-access platinum wonderpass." He grins at her. "The advantages of the frontier lifestyle. Brooklyn. Not the fancy part."

When they emerge, he leads her down a scruffy corridor to a door marked FIRE EXIT. He pushes a horizontal bar to open it. Concrete stairs lead up to another door at the top.

"Close your eyes."

Eve hears the click of the bar being pressed, and the squeak of hinges. She feels a faint breeze on her face. Micajah takes her hand lightly.

"Watch the step."

Eve feels with her foot: it's just a high lintel. She steps across it.

"Keep them closed, okay?"

"Okay."

Micajah lets go of her hand. Behind her the door creaks closed. She hears the long rasp of a zipper, things being pulled from the backpack.

"You can open them now."

They are on a wide expanse of roof, punctuated by little towers that enclose the various vents and chimneys of the building. The rooftop itself is paved with terracotta tiles. It's the tallest building in the vicinity; all around them, the sky is a haze of pink.

Micajah squats next to a spread-out blanket. On it are a couple of miniature alcohol bottles, two conical glasses, and a rather battered cocktail shaker.

"I hope you like martinis."

"I haven't had a martini in years." As soon as the words are out of her mouth, Eve regrets them. The decade since she's drunk a martini makes her feel old. Even worse is the thought that martinis are what older people drink, and that must be why he is making her one.

"Retro chic," he says. "Actually, it's just because I'm showing off. I won an award for my martini when I was bartending in Berlin a while back. I brought a bottle of white wine too, if you'd like that better."

"I'll stick with the martini," she says. "It goes with the sunset."

"Lemon or olive?" he asks, holding up two Ziplock bags.

"Both."

"Live wild," he says, bending over the drinks. His shirt has come untucked and Eve longs to tuck it back in, to feel the knobs of his spine, the vertical ridges of muscle flanking it.

He hands her a glass. She takes a small sip. Alcohol will only dull her senses, which are on fire.

He leads her to the crenellated parapet that rings the roof. She knows the architectural style: Strawberry Hill Gothic, which was used in New York only occasionally, about a century after it was popular in England. She's been studying classic English gardens for a project at the Trenton Country

Club. Her mind races to those houses: Strawberry Hill, Cholmondeley Castle. Small square windowpanes. Banks of lavender. Ranunculus. Agapanthus. She distracts herself with the complicated words, steady things to hold on to.

"Blows your mind, if you let it."

His voice brings her back. She's never considered wonder to be her choice before. Okay, she thinks: I'll let it. Right here, right now, I am on a rooftop with a crazily handsome young man who is holding my hand and showing me the view of Central Park as if he is Arthur and this is his kingdom.

Eve stares out at the expanse, a thousand colors of saturated green after a rainy spring. The sprawl of the Metropolitan Museum. The vast amounts of time and effort and imagination and ingenuity that created this city. The largesse that placed an enormous public park at its heart.

"Thank you for bringing me here," she says.

He sets his glass down on the parapet. It is a sign which, despite the decades since a man has flirted with her, she can read perfectly.

This is the time to run away, she thinks, to call it a mistake, to race back to home and safety. If I don't, home will never feel safe again.

Then that's the way it will be, she decides. Recklessness is giving her a rush more thrilling than anything she's ever felt. And there's a certainty about it, a total lack of fear. The horse is galloping, and she cannot fall off.

She sets her own glass down on the next crenellation over.

Those glasses had better not fall, she thinks. They could kill someone.

Micajah's mouth meets hers. His lips are soft and strong, pressing hers open then pulling away, an invitation to her mouth to push back against his. Instead, she draws back.

"You're young enough to be my son," she says.

"So?"

He covers her mouth again, his tongue reaching just the tip of hers, caressing her and then withdrawing, seeming to pull her tongue back along with his. She thinks: I am inside him. She has never thought that before, kissing a man. It feels delicious to follow him so closely. Her instincts flow with an ease she never knew was in her. The lead and the follow of their kissing is seamless. She feels their breath merge, the air flowing between them warmed by their bodies. He is breathing me in, she thinks. I am breathing him in. His DNA is in my veins.

His thumbs stroke her wide cheekbones, his fingers tangle in her hair, finding the edges of her ears, the tender spot where jaw meets neck, the soft indentation underneath her chin. Suddenly his lips leave hers and she feels them on the plate of bone in the center of her forehead, pressing it smooth, then tracing down the ridge of her nose, her upper lip, and dropping a chain of kisses around her mouth. She imagines a circlet of pearls that his kisses have left on her face.

She has never felt anything like this before. His lips, his tongue, his fingers, are caressing the fibers of her mind.

The stone is warm against her back, through the thin cotton of her shirt. She leans against it, freeing more of her energy to kiss him, to concentrate on the sensations of him kissing her.

What am I doing? she thinks. I am kissing this boy, this man, and soon I will be . . . fucking him? She's only ever used that word to swear with—and even then, not very often. She and Larry didn't fuck: nothing so gleeful and direct. They "had sex"—though not recently, not for years. When they were first married, less impersonally, they "made love"—though Eve had always felt rather uncomfortable with that phrase too. Did they really *make* anything together? They made a child, of course, but it was a long time between the making and the evidence of it. On that night, and every other night, Larry would climax and roll away, averting his eyes. Nothing remained that was made.

So, then, she thinks, slashing thoughts of Larry adrift, we will fuck. Maybe. It sounds good. She thinks, This should not be happening. This is not my world. But it is: his tongue is running down the cords of her neck, digging into the hollows of her collarbones. His hands are moving up under her shirt, searching for bare skin.

She trails her hand down his ribcage and back behind her, to push away from the wall and press up into him. She feels an edge, a corner—above it, empty space. The gap between the crenellations. A three-foot-wide shelf of stone.

She edges to the left, settles herself against the edge of the parapet, half sitting, and raises one knee, resting her foot against the wall. Her bent leg presses on the outside of his thigh. She puts her hands on his hips, feels the bones beneath the denim, and pulls him toward her. He stops.

Her heart flips. I don't know what I'm doing, she thinks. I've gone too far.

He draws back just far enough that she can focus on his face, see its oval shape, the tousled dark hair, those beautiful lips, dark brows shadowing green eyes like mossy pools lit by rays of sun. His eyes search hers. Here I go, she thinks, and feels herself slipping in.

He picks her up and sets her on the wall. "Eve," he says.

Her name sounds different in his voice, firm and definite. That is who I am, she thinks. Eve. The Eve who is here, hearing her name. From the mouth of this man who is about to fuck me. Under the sun and the wide sky, on a roof overlooking New York City.

She lets her sandals drop and curls the arches of her feet over the muscles of his calves.

His hands are under her skirt now, fingers tracing the lace edges of her underwear across the ridges of the tendons, then further down, further in. His thumbs press on her: a question. The energy inside her body jumps toward him.

"Yes," she says.

The lowering sun is warm on her face, glinting on the top of his dark head. She presses her hands against the parapet to lift her weight as he draws her underwear down, and gives quick silent thanks to Macy's for putting such high-end underwear on sale. She buries her gaze in the dark forest of his hair as she feels the fabric brush over her knees, across the bony points of her ankles, along the tops of her feet. Gone.

As he straightens up, he grins mischievously. The feeling of her own smile makes her think of running on the beach with Allan when he was four, chasing the waves.

"You are beautiful," he says.

"So are you."

"I'm young," he says, dismissing it. "That's all."

His hands are under her shirt again. He presses on the lowest rib, then the one above it, moving from the outside to the center, then away, up and out to the far edge of the next rib. She longs to lean back and lie open to his hands, to let him play music on her, but there is nothing behind her: only the gap between the crenellations, thin air, thirty stories above the ground. She hooks her hands tight on his shoulders.

"You're safe," he says. "I've got you."

He wraps one long arm around her back, cradling her, and with the other hand strokes her inner thigh, caressing it open. She closes her eyes and feels him touching her, finding how they fit together.

"Don't worry," he says. "I won't let go."

Her head is full of sparks, all conscious thought disjointed. The vertigo of the empty air behind her, though she can't see it; the blaze of him etching a path of fire inside her, the granite hard against her tailbone, the lean muscles of his shoulders moving under her grip, his hand cupping her breast, thumb on her nipple. I'm holding on for dear life, she thinks. If I let go, he will fuck me so hard I will fall and die.

He stops moving, buried deep inside her. "Look, Eve," he says, "look where we are."

She knows it's there, the sheer drop behind her, but seeing it—the treetops, the cars, the horse-drawn carriages—and feeling Micajah's arms holding her above the precipice sends a rush of blood to her head so fierce it makes her vision swim. She looks up, to the distant skyscrapers of Midtown gleaming pink against the indigo sky. She wonders if there's anyone behind those windows watching them—admiring them, envying them.

He starts moving again, faster, branding the blaze of pleasure deeper into her. Her whole body is concentrated in that furrow, the intensity unbearable, until she cries out and it dissolves into a new delicious heat flooding through her, out to her hips, her legs, up to her heart, her breasts, her throat, the cavities of her face. She shudders in his arms. He runs his finger up her spine.

Eventually, she opens her eyes, finds his. "What about you?"

"What about me?" he says lightly.

"But . . . are you sure?"

"But what?" he says. He smooths her eyes closed and kisses her eyelids. "Fun, right?"

What can she say? Yes, it's fun, it's beyond fun, it's not fun at all. It's crazy serious. Her body tenses up, even while the honey of orgasm flows through her.

She drops down from the parapet and slips on her sandals. He sees her eyes go to her underwear, lying on the gritty surface of the roof. He shakes it clean and holds it for her.

"I can't do this," she says, stepping into her underwear, allowing him to pull it up into place.

"I know," he says.

And again she sees that look in his eyes that dissolves the space between them.

4

On the PATH train back to New Jersey, Eve's mind and body wage exhausting war. Her limbs feel too heavy to move, as if she's been hypnotized, while thoughts crash around in her head, charging and hiding like guerrilla fighters at the crux of a battle. The thoughts wear labels, "wrong" and "right," but even so she isn't sure which side they're on. She feels hunted, her camouflage ripped away. Caught in the crossfire.

When she looked down from that rooftop, Micajah holding her tight onto him, she saw, hundreds of feet below, the Alice in Wonderland garden: the Caterpillar on a mushroom, the Mad Hatter pouring tea. What happened to her was the opposite of what happened to Alice: she had been spirited up to that high place, to a new reality above the trappings and troubles of her life, where she could bask in the rosy, unobstructed sun.

Now, heading home, she feels like she's being carried toward some monster's den. A place of torment and silently shrieking souls—hers, and Larry's too. It's suddenly clear to her how unhappy he is. And how dead to feeling she had become.

Recently she has begun to think, with the dispassion of a scientist observing a specimen, that she no longer knows what joy feels like—that sense of soaring delight in being alive that is more than mere happiness, which she came to define as merely the absence of sadness, so that she could occasionally claim it and keep her life on its tracks. If she had been asked, she would have said she was content, but now she recognizes that featureless condition for what it is: all sensation blurred into the same narcotic fog. With Micajah, she broke free of it, but here on the train, she feels it creeping over her again. Only extremes penetrate it, and they come as aggressions: so many fellow passengers that she feels as if worms are crawling over her. The platform lights so bright they hurt her eyes. A chilly wind, when she gets off, that blows her nerves to rags. The raucous laughter of a tipsy claque hopped up for a night in the city. As she drives home from the station, cars rage past her on the highway, too fast, too close.

As the garage door closes behind her, a rogue thought snipes into her brain: I could leave the engine on. For some seconds, she searches out the sweet smell of the exhaust. She imagines the atoms of her body pulling apart, the tendons and ligaments unhitching, her very self floating away. A good way to go, she thinks: a vanishing.

She snaps back to herself, clicking off the ignition. Larry's Acura is in the garage, but that doesn't mean he's home; he took a cab to the airport. There are no lights on downstairs, so if he is home he's already retreated to his room. Good—she will have some breathing space. She needs to put the day away, in a locked drawer. She'll take it out and fondle it now and then, when she's alone, but what happened today will not happen again.

She walks through the dark house to the staircase without turning on lights. A day like this should fade out, not assert its presence into the night hours.

Once, in the past, Eve thought of being unfaithful. It was nothing to do with Larry, and not much to do with the other man. It was just that the opportunity presented itself and she allowed herself to entertain the possibility.

It happened nine years ago, when Allan was a teen-ager. She was working in a client's garden, and her client's husband emerged from the house. The spring day was warm and she was wearing a sleeveless top. His hand on her upper arm, as he offered to help her dig, felt firm yet tentative: a seductive combination. The fact that the man was married—his wife and children had gone swimming for the day—was in his favor. This would be no more than a secret flirtation. He had commitments; she had no desire to jeopardize her marriage. Of course, she knew that married men—and married women—abandon their commitments all the time, but that fact seemed irrelevant. She was playing in her imagination. In the real world, it would lead nowhere.

She knew her line of logic was morally suspect, but on that

day, that month, that year, she was prepared to give herself the slack. This is how other people live, she thought, people with more exciting lives than mine.

He knelt a little too close to her and allowed his hand to brush hers as they patted the soil into place around the newly planted wisteria. If I turn my face to him now, she thought, he will kiss me and I will fall back and we will be lying on the ground, and that will not be okay. So she finished her patting and quickly stood up, brushing the earth off her hands in a manner she hoped looked professional, standing there to assess her work, which did not need assessing, instead of moving away to fetch the hose. As he got to his feet, she turned to him in a nonchalant fashion, which could easily be explained away as a prelude to conversation—if there would ever be anyone she'd need to explain it to, which in this garden with high hedges there wouldn't, which was what made this imaginary adventure possible in the first place.

He placed his hands on her upper arms. She allowed it, without protest, but without moving closer herself—keeping her route of excuses clear. As his face neared hers, she shut her eyes and thought, Here it comes. This changes me: from a boring wife into . . . What? Perhaps just a different kind of boring wife, the kind who cheats. But I am not cheating, she insisted silently. I'm just reminding myself what it feels like to be wanted.

The man kissed like a camel. When she thought about it

later, she couldn't help giggling. There was something prehensile about his upper lip. It snuffled at her. Her mind went to the camels in the zoo—when Allan was little, she'd taken him to the Bronx Zoo for four birthdays in a row—the way they scooped up tussocks of hay, their upper lips twisting and curling in a way that had struck her as almost obscene. They always looked mangy, too, with their hair (or was it fur?) falling out in tufts. She'd understood it might be due to the time of year, since Allan's birthday fell in May, but still she held it against them.

That this man was, in that way, very un-camel-like—perfectly groomed, someone who made the most of every iota of his good looks—didn't help at all. Clearly, he considered himself an excellent kisser. Maybe other women love this, she thought. She endured it until he stopped to invite her inside for a lunchtime glass of wine, which, she understood well, would be drunk, if drunk at all, naked and horizontal. No, she said, I'm so sorry, I'm running behind schedule already. The rush of walking away from him was more thrilling than the kiss.

Letting the warm water of the shower run over her, she plays back in her mind the quantum leap she took: the beautiful young man, the slow sunset, the gargoyles grinning at them, the hundreds of feet of deadly fall behind her. As the scene takes on shape and detail, it seems to be happening to another woman while she, Eve, watches from above. But she can still feel the imprint of Micajah's hands on her body, his cells on her skin. She got into the shower to wash them away. They are not going.

Eve used to like the way Larry would get up and shower after sex; she appreciated his cleanliness, and it gave her minutes of solitude, which she came to hold precious. She'd become so used to faking orgasm that she was hardly conscious of doing it anymore: moaning at appropriate intervals, digging her fingers into his back, saying his name, giving a little cry and shuddering when it was all getting long and she hoped he'd finish soon. The act had come to include the acting too. She didn't think of it as faking—simply as participating, "not just lying there," convincing herself by these sounds and movements that she did still love Larry. Yet some part of her needed to recover, to reunify her spirit without his energy there to intrude. The sound of the water while she lay in bed helped her bring her split self back together.

Now, she finds it hard to shut off the running water. As long as she stays in the shower, unable to hear the door open or the phone ring, she occupies a lacuna in time, with no demands and no necessity to corral her identity into a user-friendly package. When she turns off the water, she will have to decide who she is: a woman, with all the potential the word suggests, or a wife. She will have to accept that she has cheated on her husband, and that all effects have a cause, and all causes have effects.

I need to have more fun, she thinks aimlessly, as she waits for sleep to take her. Then I would not be so quick to lose my head.

Micajah called it fun, and she agreed. But that's not what she means, in her drowsy state. What does she mean? Bumper cars? Bridge? Line dancing? When she was twenty-two, before Allan was born, Eve might have described herself as "fun-loving," if "fun-loving" hadn't meant being what her mother called loose, an easy lay. Probably nobody uses that term these days; it sounds so quaint and innocent. It must mean "someone who loves fun" again, since there's no such thing as loose anymore. What used to be loose is normal; it's called hooking up, friends with benefits, things like that. Eve used to laugh at her mother for dividing girls into "good" and "bad," but even though the crude moral judgment seemed antiquated, there was still an uneasy distinction between girls who slept around and girls who didn't. Those who didn't, like Eve, looked down—with distaste or contempt, envy or frustration—at those who did. Those who did looked down at those who didn't with pity and maybe contempt—and, Eve realizes now, at least sometimes with envy too.

Eve feels sad for these girls, herself included, all wishing to be what they weren't. As a teenager Eve longed for a clothes-hanger body, while her flat-chested friends stuffed their bras and later went under the knife. The shy girls longing to be outgoing; the loud girls wishing they could be the hunted rather than the hunters.

Men too. Larry is a sheep who wants to be a wolf. Did I marry a sheep? Eve wonders hazily, and the thought lands like a muffled punch. Certainly she didn't marry a wolf in disguise. The wolf skin fits Larry awkwardly, but he is determined to grow into it. I need to sleep, she tells herself firmly. Count sheep. Count Larrys. She giggles, punch-drunk. Separate the sheep from the goats. Is goatish better than sheepish? Everything is better than sheepish. Larry is not goatish—that's what satyrs are: ravening for sex, hairy, dirty. Who, or what, is Larry? He gets more insubstantial by the day. It's not only that she knows him less, but there seems to be less of him there. As if he's shape-shifting himself gradually out of existence.

I am shape-shifting too, she thinks. But we can't both do it. Someone has to hold the fort. If one of us flies out too far, the other has to be the tether. That's a marriage.

"You have got to be kidding."

It's six p.m. Deborah's store is closed. Deborah herself, skinny and angular, reclines on a curvy Victorianish sofa, her bobbed white-blonde head thrown back against the gold velvet upholstery. A bottle of chardonnay sits on a fake marble column capital beside her. She sips from an antique cut-crystal glass.

"It's a beautiful decorative object."

"It's a catastrophe in a case. Even the case is a catastrophe. What the fuck, Eve?"

"I couldn't resist. It needed rescuing."

"Go volunteer at the animal shelter. Or find a therapist."

"You really don't think any of your clients would want it?" Eve is enjoying this. And so is Deborah. They both know there was never any question whether Deborah would want this broken thing.

"Honey, my store does not run on mercy bucks. Those decorator queens are flattery-operated. Every one of them wants to be told I kept back something special just for her. And if it's smashed up, it ain't special."

With her left hand she takes a swig of chardonnay, while with her right hand she tops up Eve's glass—another antique, which doesn't match Deborah's.

"Killer score on the birdcage, though."

Deborah's shop is schizophrenic. At first glance it's a conventional mix of grandmotherly furniture, silver and knick-knacks, amusing needlepoint, and a riot of cushions. Above head height it is crammed with chandeliers, some antique, some new, and some strange mutations that she creates herself out of pieces of other chandeliers, bed frames, pot racks, old gates, and birdcages, covering them with gold and silver leaf and hanging them with crystal drops, feathers, Christmas ornaments, Mexican tin *milagros*, and anything glittery she can find. Mostly she sells them online, and to interior designers from New York.

"I think it's special," says Eve.

"Well, chiquita, of course you do," says Deborah, patting her hand in a condescending way.

"Seriously. I went to the New York Public Library and I couldn't find anything like it."

"You think it could be one of those million-dollar violins that people murder each other over?"

"I don't know. Maybe."

"Any bloodstains?"

"None that I can see."

"Something sure happened, though," Deborah says with relish. "You need forensics."

"How do I get them?"

"Auction houses. Best way to get a free valuation. Sotheby's, Christie's, whoever does instruments. Google it. I get ten percent when you sell it, for my professional advice. Hell, make it fifteen. I'm worth it."

"Might only be a cup of coffee."

"Non-fat triple macchiato with sugar-free vanilla syrup and whipped cream and slivered almonds or some shit on top. Those things add up."

"Deal."

Deborah reaches over to clink Eve's glass. "Five hunting weekends in a row," she says. "Lucky me."

Even though it's summer, and unpleasant weather for junk-shop hunting. Eve should be working in her own garden on weekends—it's an advertisement for her work, after all—but the numbing fog has killed the enthusiasm she once had for making it beautiful.

"So tell me," Deborah asks with sly sarcasm, "how's that animal of a husband of yours?" Deborah laughed herself hoarse when Eve told her about Larry's discovery of his wolf spirit. She had kept it quiet for months, but one night the chardonnay got the better of her discretion.

"*Ow-ow-ow-ow-oooooo!*" Deborah howled up at a particularly bright globe chandelier. Her favorite part of the story was that Larry had found his inner wolf not in a dehydrated delirium in a Navajo sweat-lodge, or on top of a wind-blasted peak in South Dakota with blood streaming down his chest, but in a boutique bed and breakfast in New Hampshire.

Eve couldn't help laughing too, though she felt disloyal. Deborah and Larry never liked each other. He found her crass, and her swearing offended him. Eve's other friends are decorous and safe, but Eve discovered to her surprise, after meeting Deborah over the years at PTA bake sales, school plays, and graduations, that hanging out with her was a relief from saying what she ought to say and thinking what she ought to think. Having Deborah for a friend is rather like having a pet tiger: you're never quite sure when and where she will pounce. She can be exhausting sometimes, because it's hard to have total confidence that the prey she's stalking isn't you.

She's asking about Larry now because her instincts have

been pricked by Eve's abandonment of her garden. She smells blood.

"He's in Arizona," Eve says. "He's supposed to get home today."

"Supposed?" Deborah repeats. "You mean you don't know?"

"Actually, he was supposed to get home last night. I don't think he did."

Eve slept the sleep of the dead—not because she was sated from sex, but because she was emotionally exhausted by the assaults of the truth. When she woke, she listened for the usual bathroom noises, the blender, the garage door. Had he already come and gone? She might not have known, comatose as she was. Should she be worried? The distance he's forced between them in the past year has thinned her care for him.

"He didn't call?"

"No."

"Dick."

Coming to see Deborah this evening is Eve's way of asserting that everything is fine. But she came for a reality check, too. Because with Deborah, that's what you get.

"Honey, he's left you. And he's too much of a coward to tell you to your face." Deborah snorts. "Inner wolf, my ass. All that man found is his inner pussy."

"He probably just got delayed. Or there might have been an accident."

That's the first time she's said, or even thought, such a thing.

She doesn't actually believe it, but it's a way of defending Larry. Despite everything, she cannot let Deborah's accusation win the day.

"Rental cars," she adds. "They don't always check the brakes."

What began as a feint is taking shape as a horrible possibility. Eve tries to suppress the panic rushing through her veins.

"Bullshit. You'd have heard. It's not like he doesn't carry ID. Any signs of an affair? Another woman? Another man?"

You never know whether Deborah is joking or not. Another possibility made real by being voiced. Not a very likely one, but even considering it makes Eve feel unexpected sympathy for Larry, and his flailing attempts to find a place in the world more powerful than suburban husband, middling executive plodding toward retirement, boredom, obscurity, death.

Eve smiles. "No."

"That's why I love you, honey. There's not a mean bone in you, is there."

"Maybe I just haven't found it yet."

Deborah takes Eve's hand, looks into her eyes. "Don't call him, okay?"

"Okay."

"Eyes on the prize, honey. When I left Ted, I knew what was good for Deborah. You need to get on board with what's good for Eve."

She pours more chardonnay into Eve's glass, filling it to the brim.

"Now. Repeat after me: good . . . fucking . . . riddance."

Eve can't do it. He's Allan's father. He always will be.

Deborah seems to be about to say something, but doesn't. She takes a hefty swig of chardonnay, and Eve could swear it's to conceal that her eyes are damp. In a moment, her swagger is back in place.

"Shit, Eve, you're not going to wait for him like a doormat, are you? Go find yourself a tennis pro and get back into practice!"

"You know I don't play tennis."

"I don't fuck women, chiquita, but that doesn't stop me fucking a man who does."

She shouts with laughter when she sees Eve's face. Eve is tempted to tell her about Micajah. She longs to talk about him to someone, to describe his physical beauty and his spiky, unpredictable sweetness. That would turn the tables in a satisfying way. And Deborah, for all her brassy bravado, is discreet; she'll spill all her own beans, but not other people's, and unlike anyone else Eve can think of, Deborah will not judge her badly.

Not today, though. It's still too raw; the confusion of the Larry situation will leak into what happened with Micajah and mar it. Most of all, she doesn't want to turn Micajah into a story, even to entertain a close friend who, more than anyone, will cheer her on. If she tells Deborah now, it will be all about sex. Is it—was it, she mentally corrects herself—about more than that? Surely it was. Though that hardly makes it better. Is it worse to be unfaithful in the body, or in the heart and mind?

There has been no phone call from Larry, no reports of accidents on the news or on the website of the Arizona Highway Patrol. No natural disasters, hotel fires, random shootings. If he'd had a heart attack and been taken to the hospital, or been somehow hurt or killed, she'd know by now.

She has willed herself not to worry. Probably just a missed connection, and he's had to spend a day in Chicago or Kansas City or Atlanta before he could get on another flight. It's strange he has not told her, but then, these days, much of what he does is strange. She is so habituated to allowing him his moods that she cannot make Deborah's assumption that this silent absence is the end.

In fact, she's been enjoying his absence—which is only possible if she believes it to be temporary.

So the following day, at five o'clock, Eve drags on pantyhose. She loathes pantyhose at any time of year, but especially in summer. This purgatorial yearly event demands them.

It's been on the calendar for months. Larry's boss, Martin, and his wife, Eleanor, pride themselves on their common touch, and also enjoy showing off the other things they're proud of to the commoners who make up the tiers of middle management at the pill-coating company. Eve suspects that Eleanor models their summer garden party on those given by the Queen of England. It is absolutely not a pool party, despite the pool that the mingling guests have to be careful not to fall into. Waiters in white gloves interrupt boring chitchat to proffer canapés on silver trays. Some years, a string quartet has played.

Eve has never allowed herself to seriously consider bare legs for the party, just as she has never allowed herself to consider not going at all. It is her job, as Larry's wife.

The party starts at six-thirty, so there is still time. It's likely that he'll rush into the house, do a quick change, and expect her to be ready to go. Or he might take a cab directly from the airport to the party and tell her to meet him there. Five years ago, he would have been more considerate. Eve hopes the current iteration of his persona will soften soon.

While she waits, Eve sits down at her desk to write out a list of low-maintenance plants for the new county court-house complex. She smiles to herself: at least they don't want roses.

At six o'clock she checks her email: nothing. She has already left Larry two voicemails; there's no point in leaving another. As she picks up the phone to call Eleanor, who is punctilious about attendance and will expect an explanation, she notices that she is shaking.

"Eleanor, it's Eve Federman. I'm just calling to let you know that Larry and I won't make it tonight. I'm terribly sorry—a sudden illness in the family."

"Eve Federman?" Eleanor sounds as if this is a name she recognizes only dimly. "You're calling, why?"

"To let you know that Larry and I won't be there tonight."

"I'm not expecting you. Employees who have been terminated do not continue to attend company functions. Even unofficial ones."

"Terminated?" Eve feels her stomach plummet. Larry was fired, and he didn't tell her?

"Well, of course, Martin allowed Larry to save face and resign," Eleanor says into the silence. "Martin is kinder than most. It's cost him, God knows. Heavens, Eve, did you really not know?" Her queenly condescension evaporates.

Lying might salve Eve's pride, but she doesn't feel the need for that. Eleanor has just hurtled into her past; Eve doesn't care what she thinks. Knowing the truth is what's urgent.

"No. When did this happen? How long ago?"

"Eve…" Eleanor's voice gets lower, more intimate, more confiding. "It was at the pre-presentation for Stimitol—fortunately not the meeting with the client, just our own dear CEO! About three or four weeks ago, I'd say. Instead of the PowerPoint the team had worked on, Larry played some video about spirit animals! Said he was helping to *release* them. And handed out turkey feathers. Can you imagine? Turkey feathers. To all the top management! Everyone was speechless."

Eve shivers. This is the kind of story you hear about somebody else.

"I'm sure you can see, there was nowhere to go from there but out." Eleanor delivers the verdict with relish, only partly disguised by a last-minute overlay of pity for the poor, blameless wife. In fact, not quite blameless—in Eleanor's mind, or in Eve's. After all, she married him. And maybe somehow she drove him to it.

"Thank you for telling me, Eleanor." And you should thank me, Eve thinks, for giving you the punchline: *And guess what! His wife didn't know about it for weeks!*

"You're so welcome! Best of luck, Eve." She hangs up before adding, With a husband like that, you'll need it.

Eve feels panic rising in her throat. She's freezing; the air conditioning is set too high. She yanks open the kitchen door and steps into the humidity outside. It's like hitting a wall of damp cotton wool. She sinks onto the brick steps that lead down into the backyard.

Her garden might as well be a hologram. The trees, the fence, the overgrown flowerbeds, the weedy lawn: all of it, a projection of what is supposed to be her life. Only the spicy scent of lilies has the smack of the here and now.

Eve wraps her arms around her knees. Her own body comforts her: it feels solid and substantial. She runs her hands down the sides of her legs and back up along her shins. The pantyhose feels sticky: the stickiness of frogs. Her fingers stop at the bump of a small scab on her right knee. Did she do it in the junk shop, or on the roof with Micajah? She doesn't remember it bleeding that day at lunch, when she realized he was looking at her knees; she has no memory of scraping it on the roof. She presses the scab, rubs it. The fine mesh of the nylon starts to ladder. Eve digs her fingers into the hole, pulling it bigger, ripping the fabric away from her skin. Then she attacks the other leg, tearing at it until only shreds remain.

She goes back inside, barefoot, and drops the ripped panty-hose in the kitchen garbage.

This is reality, she thinks grimly. Time to face it.

She climbs the stairs and opens the door of the guest room—only the second time she's done that since Larry took it over. The first time, she went in to change his sheets and vacuum, and he asked her with cold politeness to please respect his privacy. She could have snooped while he was out, but she was too proud.

The previous night, on her way to bed, she paused at that door, wondering if the room would tell her something about Larry's absence. She knew in her gut that something was wrong, but still she could put off the moment of reckoning. She calls it ostrich pose: putting your head in the sand, refusing to see what's there. She chose to hold it for one more day.

The closet door was open that day, barely a year ago, when she entered, revealing a kind of altar, with feathers, rocks, a candle, and objects she couldn't identify. Now, when she opens the closet, she sees blank space. The altar is gone.

White wall, melamine shelving, shiny clothes rail, a few decrepit wire hangers: the objects surrounding this absence seem disconnected, like objects floating in space.

Eve sits down on the bed and tries to put herself into Larry's consciousness. What was he thinking, the last night he lay here? Did he have regrets about his intention to leave? Nostalgia? Qualms of any kind? What did he think he would say to Allan when he talked to him next? Would he even contact him? In the past, he'd always expected Eve to be the one in charge of staying in contact, and spoke to his son on cue when she handed him the phone.

What will she say to Allan? It's obvious that she will have to be the one to tell him that the solid ground of his family has crumbled away.

They were not happy, as she's finally admitted in the past days. But it never occurred to her that their individual unhappiness might implicate their marriage. The marriage itself wasn't unhappy. It was . . . She searches for the word. Normal.

Could it be another woman? No. She's pretty certain, even though certainty seems ridiculous right now. She is the one who has been unfaithful. Yet she had had no intention of being unfaithful before it happened, while he had been planning to leave her for, almost certainly, weeks. He executed his plan with clinical detachment. And all the while, she'd thought nothing was wrong.

Though she knows that more than half of marriages end

in divorce, Eve feels abnormal—abandoned, deceived, alone. This should not be happening to her and Larry. She is not flighty, not self-centered, not always looking for something better and leaving collateral damage behind her as women like Deborah do. She married Larry, with his chinos and madras shirts, because he was stable, unadventurous, kindly rather than passionate. She'd seen her parents split up, seen her mother be picked up and put down by a succession of men. Rattled by Bill's death and feeling only half alive, as if part of her had died with him, Eve was prepared to sacrifice excitement for security. Contentment seemed durable and within her control, whereas joy was transient. She vowed to lie, without complaining, in the bed she'd made.

She wanders from room to room, looking for an anchor. How can the absence of someone who has been functionally absent for so long be so pronounced?

Only one object in the house holds nothing of Larry: the instrument, which has stayed out of sight in its case since it arrived. Averting her eyes from the splintered back, she holds it in various postures: tucked under her chin, propped on her thigh, clasped between her knees. I could be a completely different person, she thinks, someone who knows how to play this. Or someone who knows how to make this. She feels herself blank, a slate wiped clean by the disappearance, physical and spiritual, of the Larry she joined her life to twenty-six years ago.

Still cradling the instrument, she sits on the sofa and stares at the blank TV. The ghost of herself looks back at her from the depths of the black screen. She's reminded of a Discovery Channel program she once saw, about Indians who looked into obsidian mirrors to learn things.

She flicks it on. The news channel is still not reporting anything that might excuse Larry's silence, though she knows by now that world events have nothing to do with it. She clicks through the channels. Men with knives. Noisy cars. Zebras on the African savanna. A nighttime rerun of a daytime talk show. Eve has never liked those shows: too much yelling and self-righteousness and exhibitionism.

"I don't know when it happened," she imagines herself saying to the host. "He moved into the guest room but we still ate dinner together."

A young woman grabs a microphone dangling from an overhead wire. "Girlfriend, you are sleepwalking! If this dude had been the Unabomber, you would have just been mashing his potatoes and never even knew it!"

A second woman grabs another microphone. "Do you even know where he is? He could be marrying a man for all you know!"

Eve stares blankly at the TV, where a soft-voiced doctor is, in fact, discussing colonic screening. The studio audience are looking concerned, enlightened, and determined. There are no dangling microphones.

Though she feels a steady, simmering anger at Larry, it's shot through with glimmers of sympathy. Could he be secretly gay, or transgender? She searches her mind for signs. Whatever the reason for his disappearance, his lying, his lack of communication, the pressure was so intense it caused what might be a psychotic break. Until now, she refused to worry about his mental state, choosing to label his behavior a phase, like the phases Allan went through as a child: tantrummy, clingy, defiant, too grown-up for his age.

There must have been signs, during those years of vague decline. And she missed them.

Until late that night, Eve attempts to compose an email to Larry, telling him she knows he's lost his job, asking what he plans to do. No combination of words sounds right: too angry, too sympathetic, too whiny, too brisk.

As she rewrites it for the twentieth time, an instant message pops up. She recognizes the phone number: Micajah.

That he should be contacting her tonight, and at two in the morning, seems outrageous. She knows it's illogical, but she holds him partly responsible for Larry's departure. It's too much of a coincidence not to be connected. The only other explanation—just as illogical, and just as unpleasant—is that fate is toying with her.

She clicks the message away. It was a bare link: probably spam, he got hacked. She tries to force her attention back to the email. Twenty-second rephrase. Twenty-third. "Please let me know if our marriage is over. Please let me know what you plan to do about our life together." She cannot send these. They are absurd.

She retrieves the message, clicks it open. There's the link, some incomprehensible code. And after it, "xM".

He let two days pass before he contacted me. Eve tries to summon outrage—anything but desire, tenderness, hunger for his body, the green depths of his eyes . . . thoughts that don't belong here, in this moment, when she's trying to throw a line over the abyss to her wayward husband.

If it's spam, a virus might take out her computer. But she's lost so much, what would it matter losing more? She trusted Micajah to hold her on that parapet; she will trust him now.

She clicks on the link. A small window pops up, with a "Play" arrow. She clicks again.

Three plaintive notes: a single melody line, played on a low-sounding violin. It's in waltz time, lilting and yearning. The notes slide together woozily, as if they're slightly drunk. She imagines Micajah's long fingers pressing the strings, bent into a caress around the bow, in perfect control of this delirious melody. His eyes are closed, she thinks, as he plays; she longs to see him like that, his face abandoned to her gaze. For nearly four minutes, the music circles and dances, conjures longing and ecstasy.

As the last note, a keening cry, fades away, a title pops up: "Night Blooming Jasmine." And then the words, "For Eve."

5

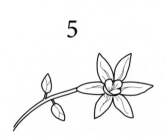

The melody haunts Eve. She wrote back only "Thank you," nine quick strokes. She couldn't face another compositional task, like the email to Larry.

In the end, Larry emailed before she managed to come up with anything she felt good about sending. "Dear Eve," he wrote, "You need to know that I'm going to be staying in Arizona for a while. I don't give a shit about pill coatings. I need to do work that feeds me. I've taken a job as head of web development for Blaine." The spirit-animal guru. "I was waiting to see if I got the job before letting you know. Blaine went out last night to make sure he was making the right choice. His spirit animal is a javelina. Arizona is three hours behind New Jersey, so that's why it took so long." It was unsigned.

Eve hardly knew what to make of it. The unnecessary, jumbled facts; the lack of apology or any evidence of remorse; the total absence of emotion; the ambiguity about whether his departure is temporary or permanent. If it doesn't work out, does he expect to just pick up this life again where he left it?

She imagines him typing "Sorry for the silence, love Larry"

and deleting it, since a wolf would not apologize. She cannot believe that he wouldn't at least have thought those words.

Her mind is whirling. Can a marriage end this way? Just stop, without even a whimper?

A follow-up email, a few hours later, details their savings: stocks, IRA, investment account, and the heavy borrowings against them. He informs her that he will be opening a new bank account. He does not mention the house or the mort-gage or any intention of helping her with the bills.

The passive-aggressiveness of this sends Eve into a fury. They were a team, a unit, as long as it suited him; now that he's found himself a new identity, all that has been tossed away. Yet even so, he's keeping his options open, dodging the decision of divorce or no divorce. If he forces her to make it, later he can throw it back in her face.

So she won't make it, at least not for now, despite the waves of rage and disgust that sweep over her. But she takes off her ring and stashes it in a drawer of her dressing table, wonder-ing how much the gold in it is worth. And she emails Allan, asking him to call her. This is the kind of news that has to come with the warmth of a living voice.

"I'm not sure how to say this, honey," she begins, "but I think your dad has left me."

Silence, then Allan repeats, with emphasis, "You think?"

"He didn't say it, in so many words. Just that he's staying in Arizona. But he's taken half the money from our savings, so that seems pretty clear."

"Wow."

"Yeah. Wow is right."

"Are you okay, Mom? When did this happen?"

"Yesterday. And yes, I'm fine."

"Really?"

The concern in his voice brings tears to her eyes, tears that Larry could not make her cry.

"Yes, sweetheart. Really."

"Good."

There's a silence on the other end. She imagines Allan, in his calm, deliberate way, rolling out the meaning of it all.

"I'm sorry, Allan. I never wanted this to happen."

"I know, Mom. You'd have gone to your grave pretending everything was fine, but it wasn't. I was hoping you guys would work it out. But if you couldn't, then you know? I'm glad. I hated seeing you like that. You and Dad both."

That astounds her. Until this moment, she's thought of the failure of their marriage as exactly that: a failure. Her failure, and Larry's. As Allan talks, level-headed and comforting, the separation sounds more like an achievement. Which, strangely, she will have to credit to Larry.

She feels her skin go cold. What if Allan asks whether Larry has been having an affair? It wouldn't occur to him that she might be the one with a lover. Even if she answers truthfully, she'll feel like she's lying. Thank God he doesn't.

"I love you, Mom. You're strong and you're brave. Maybe you don't feel strong right now, but I know you will."

"Thank you, honey," she says, longing to hold him again, to feel his thick hair, and the way he clasps both her hands in his, which reminds her of Bill.

When they hang up, her mind drifts back to that surge of panic and relief. How can she possibly tell her son that she has a lover only four years older than him? Maybe she will never have to, but that doesn't feel right either. A lie of omission is almost as bad as one baldly told.

As the days pass, that qualm is overcome. She spent mere hours with Micajah—they meant nothing in the scheme of her life with Larry. His course of departure was already set. And they will mean nothing in her future—whatever that is.

Best of all are the mornings.

It wasn't just that Larry left the bathroom door open, so that she could hear what he probably thought of as the manly, or wolfish, stream of his piss. He had a whole array of morning noises: snorts and hacking gargles, followed by loud spitting and blowing his nose into the sink (which he did an inadequate job of cleaning up). This was thanks to the guru, who had borrowed from Ayurveda the practice of clearing the *ama*, the toxic residues that accumulate overnight, and added to it an animal's lack of delicacy about bodily functions. Hardly surprising, Eve thinks, luxuriating in her peaceful house, that men find his philosophy so irresistible: it gives them permission to do all the things their mothers tried to drill out of them.

In the last year, Larry had also begun to let out his belches and farts full blast. She's not sure she can blame this on the guru; she suspects it was Larry's own coded fuck-you. I will not repress myself for you, they said; I will not apologize for being physically present in this room. She knows he blamed her for the end of their sex life, even though it seemed to come about by mutual agreement, or rather, mutual apathy. His inner wolf was not unbridled enough to actually rape her, on the rare occasions when he might have wanted to; he probably also considered this insufficient alpha-ness her fault.

Still, she cleaned his bathroom, bought his food, cooked his meals, did his laundry, thinking that making his life easy would satisfy him. In reality, she sees now, she just made herself his housekeeper.

When she listened for Larry's noises and didn't hear them, the silence was a chink that she could slip through unnoticed and find a few hours of freedom. This silence feels like a vast expanse of open country, with no walls or fences to hem her in. As the day ages, agoraphobia sneaks up on her. In her low moments, the wide-open spaces of her new single life are more like a windswept desert, studded with question marks like saguaro cactuses. Known misery felt safer than this.

Her panics focus on money—that, at least, is a subject she can tackle. Larry's mid-level corporate job insulated her from worry, but it didn't leave much extra. The only income she can rely on now is whatever she can make from her garden design business. Looking back, she sees that she took it about as seriously as an eight-year-old takes her lemonade stand. She's going to have to amp it up, fast. She makes a list of architects to meet with and public and professional buildings with landscaping that needs help—certain, though, that none of this will happen soon enough.

She finds herself buying fat loaves of ciabatta, stopping at an anonymous Italian restaurant for a plate of fettuccine Alfredo, ordering a scone with her latte. The doughiness is like padding around her. It blunts the sharp edges of reality, and of her own thoughts.

When she weighs herself on Saturday, the scale shows an extra three pounds. I am sinking, she thinks. I'm pretending I'm holding it together, but I'm not.

There is one, long-shot chance: the instrument. She joked to Deborah that it could be worth thousands. What if she was right?

Eve makes her way through the display rooms of the auction house, which is lined with paintings under individual spotlights and sculptures on plinths. The effect is plush at first glance, threadbare at second: it conveys both money and thrift. We will sell your property for thousands, maybe millions, it whispers, but our commission barely covers the cost of carpeting.

A few brawny men are heaving crates and canvases in and out. Hope flashes through Eve that she might see Micajah: he said that his day job involved moving art. Even if she can't see his face—even if she sees him from behind—she will recognize the lanky frame, the unruly dark hair, the fine strength of his arms and hands.

But he isn't there. Of course, he wouldn't be. He said he worked for a gallery. Galleries do their own selling, don't they?

Down a hallway, the carpet gives way to linoleum, the warm spotlights to cold fluorescents. A strange mix of people mill in front of a long, high counter, carrying an even stranger mix of items: paintings and etchings, pottery both beautiful and hideous, primitive artifacts. The ones carrying jewelry are easily identifiable by their furtive looks, as if the jewelry they want to sell is hot, which maybe it is.

A young woman emerges. The pillowy bouclé of her jacket announces it's genuine Chanel. She isn't buying those clothes on the wages she makes here, Eve thinks idly. This is the kind of job rich girls do to kill time and make contacts before marrying well and joining the board of the Met. She doesn't want to touch the case. It still has the stink of an ethnic junk shop on it.

"Leave it with me, please," she says. "You can collect it at five. We close at five-thirty. We'd appreciate it enormously if you'd be prompt."

She disappears through a door which a uniformed porter holds open for her, carrying the instrument at arm's length. Eve almost admires the magnificently rude politeness with which she's been dismissed. That inbred sense of superiority is something Eve will never possess. She imagines the girl at six years old, ordering something princessy from a maid: fresh strawberry juice, maybe, spiked with the blood of butterflies.

Eve is at a loose end for the day. She could go to the Public Library, but that seems silly. The instrument is in the hands of an expert, who will tell her more in five minutes than she could research in five months. The Metropolitan Museum? She's already been through the instrument room, and it's summer so the main galleries will be crowded. Back to the outer boroughs? But she's dressed to look like someone who sells expensive items at auction; these are not clothes for bargaining in.

As she turns to go, she notices a pile of art magazines on a side table. On a whim, she sits in a plastic chair and leafs through one. It's full of ads for contemporary art galleries. That's probably the kind of art that Micajah moves, she thinks: that's what the oligarchs and criminal billionaires buy. She's seen pictures of Jeff Koons pieces in *Time*—giant shiny toys in pink and silver—and didn't get the point. It's time to broaden her mind.

The streets of the West Teens are eerily quiet. There is little foot traffic, few cars or cabs. Nobody lives here; in daytime, at least, nobody shops here. The place seems to exist purely on its own fumes, requiring no sustenance from beyond its borders.

Eve expected the galleries to be like stores, with window displays that she could study and learn from, but mostly the windows are frosted or painted white, and the names of the dealers are so discreet they have to be hunted for. Some fronts have no name at all, and no windows. If you don't know who we are, they say, we don't want you.

Eve's senses are on hyper-alert for Micajah. She tells herself that she didn't come here hoping to bump into him; she came to see the art. She dares to enter a gallery with blanked-out windows. Inside is a cavernous space, with more attendants than artworks. A trio of twenty-something girls give her the same disdainful look in triplicate. Like the girl in the auction house, their clothing—in this case radical, downtown, artsy, daring—is a calculated offensive weapon, garments that differentiate the wearer from everyone who is not as rarefied as they are. Eve's natural shape would always have disqualified her from their company.

It's cold in this gallery. The concrete floor and white walls remind her of a mausoleum. The few artworks in sight are displayed with a reverence that makes her think of idols worshipped by an extraterrestrial tribe in a science fiction movie: harshly spotlit, protected by these fabulously dressed guardians with their icy stares. She imagines they have some acrid green liquid running through their veins.

She cannot picture Micajah in this company. He is nothing like them.

It's a relief to be outside again. There is a van parked down the street, a couple of men moving crates out of a building. Her heart leaps at the possibility that Micajah might be one of them. What she would do if she saw him, she's not sure: disappear into a doorway, maybe. She wants him to be the one to catch sight of her, to call her name, to be delighted to see her. She walks with her eyes casually averted, as if she is lost in thought or admiring the art—that won't work as an excuse, though, since there's so little of it to be seen. A dialogue plays out in her head, as if she's being cross-examined on a witness stand; she needs excuses, needs to be able to claim innocence of contacting him again. If she is the defendant, who is the plaintiff: Larry? Micajah? Both? Neither?

She does not hear Micajah call her name.

For a moment, she worries that the reason for this is that he deliberately ignored her; he's had second thoughts, he's embarrassed by what happened between them and has wiped her from his consciousness. But, no, it's simple—he didn't call her name because he isn't here. There are thousands of galleries in Manhattan. He may not be working today. He may not even move art anymore, now that his record deal is signed. An imp in her brain prods her with the thought that maybe it's not even called a record deal anymore, since nobody makes actual records. His world is another world in which she doesn't belong.

She walks west, toward the Hudson. There is a kayaker out there, playing with the current: fighting his way upstream, then spinning on the nose of his boat and letting the water speed him south. She watches him for what might be half an hour. Seagulls wheel overhead. She manages to adjust her hearing, change foreground for background, so that the seagulls drown out the roar of traffic on the West Side Highway.

She decides to walk back uptown to the auction house. She keeps a steady pace, which makes her feel strong and confident. Still, she finds herself glancing into the faces she passes, hoping that among the millions she will see the one face she craves.

She doesn't. It's a good thing, she tells herself. I am rebuilding my life, and I cannot rebuild it with him.

"Extraordinary."

Does he mean that the instrument itself is extraordinary, or that it's extraordinary that anyone could have the gall to waste his time with it? The expert's tone could convey either. He wears a tweed suit that is foppish rather than academic, with a pale aquamarine pocket square and no tie. The skin of his throat is yellow and bumpy, like a chicken's.

"Extraordinary piece. I must ask how it came to be in your possession."

"I bought it in a secondhand store in the Bronx. It was shoved away in a corner when I found it."

He examines her face, gimlet-eyed, as if this is an obvious lie. The case is on the high countertop between them, lying open.

"It's badly damaged." This is said in an accusatory tone, as if Eve had smashed the instrument herself.

"I know."

"That makes it unsaleable."

"I thought you might say that."

"However, the damage is, thank Jupiter, confined to the reverse. An expert repair . . ." He shrugs. "But an expert repair, I beg you. Not a botch job." His voice quavers.

Despite herself, Eve feels a glimmer of pity for him. He's an odd creature who doesn't belong here, and he has made himself odder in order to claim his space.

"And if I did get it repaired?"

He stares at her. "Damn the expense?"

"That's not possible."

"I see. You could perhaps induce someone to fund it, with the promise of a percentage of the proceeds. A business proposition."

"I would need your estimate," Eve says.

"Sadly, that is something I cannot give you until I see the quality of the repair."

"Assuming an expert repair. Please. It doesn't have to be on paper."

"Hmm." He probes around the edges of the instrument. "Restored. With wood of the right vintage, original materials, animal glue . . ."

He leans close, and whispers in her ear. "Six figures, I would suggest. With the right competition, of course."

Eve gasps.

"You have, I am sure, heard of the great composer Antonio Vivaldi, who was choirmaster of a girls' school in eighteenth-century Venice. It was, in fact, an orphanage. Naturally, you are aware that orphanhood does not discriminate between the sexes. So there were boys' orphanages as well, with similar music masters, and the boys were taught trades. One became luthier to the doge. There's no question in my mind that he is the master craftsman who made this. For, I would guess, the Ottoman court, by whom he is known to have been commissioned. The jasmine suggests an Oriental client. That particular instrument, which history records as a viola d'amore of elaborate design, is considered lost. A case could be made that this is it."

Eve's head is spinning.

"Your next question is, can I recommend a restorer. Here is the name of a man in Paris. His English is excellent. He communicates by electronic mail." He gives her a card.

"I've been told about a restorer here, named Yann Logue," Eve says. "Do you know of him?"

The expert's face tightens. "His work is excellent. However, I cannot recommend him."

"Why not?"

He snaps the clasps of the case shut, and gives Eve a slight bow before disappearing through the door behind the counter, leaving her question unanswered.

Paris. Even if the man does communicate by email, she will have to take the instrument there personally. There's no way she can afford that, under present circumstances. And she knows nobody who might be willing to fund such a repair. Nobody who can help her at all—except Micajah.

He has been sending one text a day: a photo of a jacaranda tree in blossom, remarking that he wishes one would grow in Brooklyn; a video clip of elephants mourning their dead; lines of poetry by Hafiz and John Donne. At first, she didn't reply because of her better-or-worse commitment to her marriage. Then, because of the absurdity of such a relationship, the impossibility of explaining it to Allan. Besides, she does not want to run from one man to another, distracting herself from Larry's absence with fantasies of a future with Micajah. They have no future. She should accept the universe's verdict, as given in the gallery district, and never see him again.

And after a week of no replies, his messages stopped.

When Micajah gave her Yann Logue's number, he said he did not want her to feel beholden to him. Surely he cannot mind if she calls it. However she looks at her situation, this man is her only hope. How difficult can he be? She is willing to offer him a generous deal: half of the proceeds. Surely he cannot say no to that.

So, the following day, during business hours, she phones Yann Logue. He listens as she describes the instrument and its damage. Then she tells him what the expert at the auction house said, and makes her offer.

He flies into a rage. "Instruments are for making music, not for making money! You find this lovely creature which has suffered so, and you want me to clean it up before you put it on the block, like a slave stolen from Africa and made to sing? You make me sick!"

"Please, Mr. Logue—" Eve starts.

"Do you even care what it sounds like? No. You care only to find some vampire millionaire who will suck out its soul. Parasites, all of you!"

He slams down the phone. Eve clicks off, shell-shocked.

6

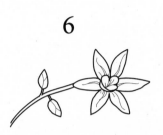

The thought of those six figures loops through Eve's days. The end to her worries: a couple of years to find her financial feet, to support her while Larry is gone, and maybe beyond. She does not know what she will do if Larry comes back saying, I'm sorry, it was all a mistake. Her throat constricts when she thinks of him returning; she would lose this new sense of air in her days. On the other hand, it's hard to imagine the rest of her life without him; she hasn't had enough practice yet. And on the third hand, even if he did return and they found some way to carry on together-yet-not, she does not want to be financially dependent on Larry again.

The only way forward is forward, Eve's mother used to say. Even if you don't know where you're going, take the next step you see, and then the next, and one day you'll find yourself in the sunlight.

"Micajah? It's Eve calling."

"I know."

"I'm sorry for my silence."

"Did I scare you?"

He doesn't sound angry. Maybe this won't be as hard as she feared.

"It wasn't you," she says, stumbling over her thoughts. "It was me. I scared myself."

Eve tried to prepare for this call by running through various potential dialogues. The process brought her the opposite of clarity. In the thicket of scenarios that sprang up, she lost her way—lost her sense of who Micajah is, lost her own emotional compass. The only solution, she decided, when she finally built up the courage to phone him, is to throw away the words that keep rehearsing themselves in her head. If it goes badly, at least she'll have been honest.

Still, she's hoping that she won't have to tell him about the mud pit her life has suddenly become. She does not know whether seeing him again would drag him into it or catapult her out of it. In any case, her marital status was probably part of her attraction; the strings that she came attached to could not attach to him. She will approach him as a friend, without expectations of romance, and hope that he will meet her in that neutral space.

"I called to ask you for help."

"I thought you didn't want it."

"I didn't know what I wanted. Or needed," she says. "But things have changed."

"How?"

There's no way around it.

"My husband left me."

She hasn't spoken those words out loud, to anyone, until this moment. She can hear Micajah absorbing the information.

"It wasn't because of you," she adds. "It had nothing to do with you—with you and me—at all."

"Good."

"He doesn't know."

Silence falls, but the connection between them is palpable. Eve feels it as a channel along which words will flow without obstruction as long as they are transparent as water, clean of blame.

"It wasn't my intention to blow your life apart," Micajah says at last. "At least, not in that way."

"I know."

"So what's the help?" His voice is lighter. He didn't apologize, and she's glad.

"I need to sell the instrument. Apparently, it's worth a lot of money, if I get it fixed."

"Did you call Yann?"

"He was—" How to say it? "Pretty dismissive. Rude. I know you said not to take it personally, but it was personal."

"You told him you planned to sell it?"

"That's the only way I'd be able to pay him."

"He doesn't care about money."

"That was obvious."

"This isn't his world. He should have lived back when it

took sixty years and three generations of craftsmen to make a viola da gamba."

Micajah, too, maybe. With his physical beauty and his talent, the world lays itself out for him. But she has the sense that he's more comfortable unseen, in the spaces between things. Unlike his father, he leaves a light footprint.

"I'm sorry," he says. "I should have insisted on taking it to him myself."

"Would you?"

A pause. Then: "Maybe we should find somebody else."

She hears the "we" louder than the wariness. Somehow, they are in this together.

"There isn't anybody else. Not in this country. That's what the expert at the auction house said. He gave me the name of a guy in Paris."

"Then let's go to Paris."

He took the leap, just as she knew he would as she was saying the words. If only she could say yes.

Eve and Larry spent their honeymoon in Paris. It was her choice—he would have preferred something involving golf and a pool with a swim-up bar. He had dutifully trailed her around the Louvre and Notre Dame and Montmartre, and at night on the Pont Neuf with the moonlight glittering on the Seine, she had the feeling that this was how it was supposed to be when you were young and in love and in Paris, and they'd kissed and gone back to their down-at-heel hotel, which Eve insisted was romantic since it was the kind of place where

Hemingway and Henry Miller and other broke writers and artists would have lived, and let Paris infuse its magic into them.

"Eve…" Micajah says. His voice has a sandblasted quality. "Meet me again."

Micajah has no need of her that she can discern, no obvious reason to pursue her. That he wants her in his life lifts her self-image to a place that makes her uncomfortable even as it thrills her. Why me, she wonders again, with twenty years and twenty pounds too much on me? Twenty-three, she corrects herself, after a week of comfort through carbohydrates.

She recognizes his body before she can see his face: long legs draped over the convex surface of a mushroom, narrow torso propped up by one arm. She has never been so acutely aware of a man's body before.

It was Micajah who suggested the Alice in Wonderland garden. Though it reminds Eve of their adventure on the rooftop—everything about Micajah reminds her of that—a children's playground will tone down the sexual charge between them. Any kids there will serve as chaperones.

As she walks toward the garden, she sees that there are no kids. It's late afternoon; it must be uptown children's dinnertime—early, so that the nanny can leave for the evening. The only person there is Micajah. She feels her body responding to his eyes: a lilt in her walk, a looseness in her hips that she didn't intend. She wonders if he expects them to come together as lovers. She cannot walk casually up to this beautiful creature and accept, as if it were normal for them, his lips on hers.

"Eve," he says, "it's good to see you."

He helps her up onto the mushroom, grasping her wrist so that she can grasp his, like a linked chain. He slides his hand lightly down hers, to hold it, but moves no closer. He is not going to kiss me, Eve thinks, with a relief that is instantly smothered by yearning.

"This is my favorite garden," he says. "At least, one of. I want to hear about yours."

So they're not going to talk about Larry, or Yann—not yet. Micajah has placed the starting blocks in a neutral zone.

"All my favorites are in England," she begins. "I like gardens that look like they've been made by someone who loves flowers, where the flowers are just abundant and glorious and taking over the earth."

"So you're not big on the French thing. Patterns and symmetry and lots of beige sand."

She laughs. "Not really. Too much control. I can admire them, but I can't love them."

"I get that."

She tells him about a garden tour through England, her one major trip without Larry. The giant banks of lavender at Hidcote; the stone terraces half-taming the wild hillside below Haddon Hall. The last stop was Port Eliot in Cornwall, an estate threaded with grassy paths and hidden dells and, near the river, a high privet maze. When the group broke up and everyone wandered separately, their paths crossing with random suddenness, a rogue thought came to her: this is the perfect garden for an orgy. She could almost see it: people wearing opulent, half-undone clothes chasing one another by moonlight through that tamed wilderness, rolling together in the little dells sheltered by flowering bushes.

She can imagine being there with Micajah—in another lifetime.

"Tell me about your own garden. I want to know your favorite thing about it."

Eve thinks of her backyard, her house, her loss of connection to them both. She's been living there like a tenant—the way she was living in her marriage.

"I'll tell you the garden I'd love to make, more than anything."

"Okay," he says, leaning back again. "Bait and switch. Distract me."

"I'd make a flower clock."

Eve has only recently learned about flower clocks; she hasn't considered actually making one until just now. But the desire is real. Micajah's interest is like a lens that focuses the rays of her own.

"What's a flower clock?"

"Linnaeus, the great botanist, had this idea that you could tell the time by what time of day flowers open and close."

"Did he make one?"

"Nobody knows."

"Did anyone? Is it even possible?"

"I don't know. I'm still researching it."

"Hard to know where to look," he says thoughtfully. He's not just making conversation; he's thrown himself into the idea.

"Linnaeus made a list of plants, but that was for Sweden. If you were making a flower clock at a lower latitude, you'd have to change at least some of them."

"My mom has a friend who planted a herb garden in the shape of a clock," Micajah says. "I always thought it looked like a pizza. But I like the idea of flowers blooming like a slo-mo Mexican wave."

"Linnaeus arranged them like a sundial," Eve says, "but I think that's part of why it didn't work—if he tried it at all. Plants like different conditions: the type of soil, the amount of water, sun and shade. It's hard to do that if they're so close together. You could use pots, but that feels like cheating."

"Why?"

"Maybe for Linnaeus it wouldn't have been. For me . . . It's hard to explain."

"Try. I'm good at this kind of thing."

"What kind of thing?"

"Understanding baffling concepts that make no sense to anybody but the person who has them." He places his finger in the crook of her elbow. "I already know you don't cheat."

"Actually, you know the complete opposite," she says slowly, feeling that she no longer knows herself.

"No. What you did—what we did—was absolutely true. That was *you*."

He's right. Looking back from the perspective of that rooftop, it's her life with Larry that was, in larger and larger proportion, a lie.

"If I made a flower clock, you wouldn't even know that's what it was," says Eve, pulling the conversation back to safety. "I'd make it in a little walled garden, just big enough so that some plants could have sun and some could have shade, and they could all have whatever kind of soil, and amount of water, they need."

"And you'd lie in the center and watch the clockwork of the cosmos in action. Time dancing all around you."

Eve imagines Micajah lying there, long legs in thick, cool grass, an arm shading his eyes against the sun, the work of her hands surrounding him. She has never had that vision of herself, never thought of the moment when the work stops and she simply enjoys it.

"It seems like it would change every day," he says, "with the days getting longer or shorter."

"It would probably only work for one day a year. Which is why it would take so long to get it right."

"Only if you wanted it to tell the exact hour. If you were trying to be really human and controlling. Or you could see it as a relativity clock. You could call it the Einstein Garden."

Outside the railings of the garden where they sit, a group of men are taking off their business suits to reveal Lycra workout gear. One brings out a hanger from his briefcase and hangs his suit from the branch of a tree. Another man jogs up, ripped T-shirt showing off his ripped torso, and fist-bumps the man who brought the hanger. He greets the one man still wearing his suit with a slap on the shoulder. The man winces.

The man who hung his suit on the tree drops and does a few ostentatious push-ups. He stares at Micajah and Eve reclining on their mushroom pedestal, a curl of judgment at the corners of his mouth. Eve feels as if every age line on her face is etched in acid.

"Can I recite some poetry to you?" Micajah says.

"Sure." She shifts position, turning her face away from the men outside the railings.

"It's in French."

"I don't speak French. Only a few words."

"Doesn't matter. You'll understand. It goes with this place." He waves at the playground and smiles at her. "I'm actually half French. But it's not my gardening half."

The electricity between them is a steady glow, rather than a jolting disturbance. Eve settles into it, letting the outside world drop away.

"*Il brilgue, les toves lubricilleux se gyre en vrillant dans le guave . . .*"

The rhythm is familiar, but Eve doesn't quite recognize it.

"*Enmimé sont les gougebosqueux, et les môme rathes hors-grave.*"

Her face lights up. "'Jabberwocky'?"

"I knew you'd get it. I don't know why I find the French version so funny."

"It just sounds so French."

"Prissy and tight-assed, you mean?"

She laughs. "You said it, not me."

"You can't offend me." He kisses her on the mouth. Her frail defenses shatter.

Of course she knew this would happen. Of course it wasn't just about finding a restorer for the instrument. She saw his face come closer with the exaggerated clarity of the milliseconds before an accident: all the time in the world to think and brace for the impact, and no time at all to evade it. Even if she'd wanted to.

As their faces part, she sneaks a glance at the Lycra-clad businessmen, wondering if they're watching.

They're not. They're all on their hands and knees, intently searching the ground and tearing up fistfuls of weeds. The leader struts among his pupils, holding a stopwatch.

"Do you know what they're doing?" she asks Micajah.

"That," he says, "is the species *Homo ubercapitalensis* preparing for the apocalypse, by learning how to survive on the wild bounty of Central Park. They're fitting it in between meetings. Behold a failed evolutionary experiment in progress: a short burst of glory and exploitation, followed by extinction."

Robert, Micajah's father, would fit in well among them, she thinks.

"We can hope, anyway," adds Micajah.

Nearest to them is the older man still wearing his suit. He's moving awkwardly, shoulders slumped in defeat, empty-handed.

"Only thirty more seconds, Jerome," barks the leader, Reebok-ed feet barely twelve inches from the man's nose. "Forage or you'll starve!"

The man looks around as if hoping for support that he cannot quite specify. Eve's heart goes out to him. She slides down off the mushroom and scans the ground.

"That's borage," she says, loudly enough for him to look at her, pointing to a broad-leaved weed growing between the railings. "It's actually really tasty." She spots something else. "And that's sorrel." Seeing a reddish, creeping plant between the paving stones of the garden, she picks it and hands it to him through the bars. "And this is purslane."

"My wife wants me to do this," he says, taking the purslane from Eve. "Our daughter is marrying him." He tips his head toward the leader.

There's a lifetime's worth of misery in the man's eyes.

She feels his pain like a whip. Grabbing her handbag from the mushroom she forces herself to say to him, "Good luck," and virtually runs out through the gate.

She hears Micajah's footsteps behind her, catching her up. "Eve, what's the matter?"

She doesn't slow down until she's a few hundred yards from the garden, and the foragers are out of sight.

"I couldn't stand it," she says, fighting back tears that she can't explain even to herself. Micajah folds her in his arms. She rests her hand on his shoulder, and feels his heartbeat against the collarbone under her fingers. Her agitation ebbs away.

Her face nestled in his neck, she inhales his cinnamon-salt smell, feels the velvet softness of his skin there. She presses closer, their abdomens touching. Stealthily, she moves her leg between his; tall as he is, he has had to spread them apart to get low enough to hug her well. Just barely, she touches the inside of his thigh with the outside of her own.

She feels him stir against her, light as a breath of wind. An intense happiness surges in her. She has done this to him. His body is responding to her thought—and his thoughts are hijacked. It makes her feel beautiful.

She cannot remember, with Larry, a moment of pure tenderness that turned, like this, into desire. They had made out, of course, and she'd felt him grow hard, but though it was the known next beat in their stumbling dance, it was somehow embarrassing and they'd rushed over it to the act of sex, which, though embarrassing too, carried its own momentum and a tacit agreement that it would not be talked about afterward.

"I don't want to be your boyfriend," Micajah says into her ear. "I want to be your lover."

A thrill runs through her. What's the difference? A boyfriend is stable, socially acceptable. A lover suggests only sex—not even love. No commitment, no tomorrow. A crystallization of time, like the garden she talked of making.

She's not sure she can do it.

"Where shall I take you?" he asks.

"Anywhere."

"Brooklyn?"

His place.

"We could stop and get takeout," he says.

This is the step that will bring her into the sunlight—as long as she's strong enough not to care how big the patch of sunlight is or how long it will last. She will be agreeing to premeditated sex with a man she barely knows, someone shockingly unsuitable who has already shredded her self-control—yet who makes her feel, when she is with him, like herself, in a way she cannot recall ever feeling before.

She remembers her mother hanging out five children's worth of laundry on the clothesline in their backyard, the tired corners of her mouth weighing down her smile. What would she say? Eve is suddenly overcome by a longing that her mother could have taken a lover, seized even an hour purely for herself.

"Okay." She smiles. "Chinese."

Fate has given her a gift. In honor of her sacrificed, sacrificing mother, she will allow Micajah to break her heart.

7

The warm spring air lifts Eve's skirt as they ride toward Brooklyn on Micajah's Vespa. He zigzags from avenue to street to avenue, in and out of the low sun's shadow. When they pick up speed, she feels the wind stroke her legs, from the bones on the outsides of her knees up her thighs and down to her ankles. At first she balked at wearing the helmet he gave her, wanting to feel the wind in her hair—and wondering, too, if he carries it because he has a girlfriend or if he's just always prepared for one. But as they ride, she glories in the invisibility. In the unlikely event that someone she knows sees them, they will not know it's her.

She has never ridden pillion before. In the first few turns, as the bike dipped to one side, she clutched Micajah's waist, but soon she relaxed and her hands dropped to his hips, her index fingers resting along the leather belt beneath his loose shirt. As she leans in, mirroring his movements, she feels in sync with the universe, dancing with gravity and centrifugal force.

To her left, the full moon hangs low in the east, wan above the sea of artificial light that washes out the stars. Eve feels a kinship, as if the moon shares her pleasure in seeing and not being seen. As the Vespa hits a run of green lights heading south, the moon flickers like an antique clip of film, visible only when they pass a cross street, calm and fixed in the lavender sky.

When they turn onto the Brooklyn Bridge, the moon looms in front of them as if it is their destination.

They wind through increasingly derelict and deserted streets, punctuated by corner bodegas. Micajah stops in front of a large steel door, kicks down the stand and takes off his helmet.

"I told you it wasn't the fancy part," he says, as Eve shakes her head clear. She feels like a sailor who has to find her land legs again.

He unlocks a padlock, slides the door open, and wheels the Vespa inside. The door clangs shut behind them.

They walk up flights of concrete stairs and down passage-ways lit by naked bulbs. Finally, they reach another industrial door with a hasp and a padlock. Once it's open, he flips off the staircase light before switching on the lights inside. That moment of darkness is another break between her old self and the new.

"It used to be a lace factory," he tells her. "I chose it for the windows."

Windows line three sides of the cavernous space, here and there shaded by lengths of hanging silk in rich colors.

"Secondhand saris," says Micajah. "I had a girlfriend who

did set dec for fashion shoots. She taught me to shop in Indian neighborhoods."

Will he say one day that he had a girlfriend who designed gardens? And taught him . . . what? Eve feels a sense of vertigo. To reach the position of girlfriend, and then ex-girlfriend— each one requires a fall.

He sets the takeout boxes on the kitchen counter, and disappears into a far corner. Eve hears a clanking of pipes, then the sound of water rushing into a bath.

"Okay?" he says as he comes back toward her across the acreage of tightly laid hardwood floor. He is already barefoot.

She returns his smile. "Yes."

It's frightening, though. The track lights will show up every sag and crease and cellulite dimple on her body.

"How hungry are you?" he asks. "Dinner before bath, or after?"

"After," Eve says. Her appetite has vanished and, in her state of unease, she is comforted by the promise of a detour between bath and bed. If he changes his mind and doesn't want to go to bed at all, it will be easier that way.

He takes her hand and leads her to the bath. The wall partitioning it off is made of hundreds of framed photographs hanging from the ceiling on ribbons of duct tape, like heavy bead curtains. Each black-and-white photo shows a group of people, seated and standing, from six or eight to many dozen, in Arabic-looking robes or fezzes and high-collared suits, formal in their strangeness and touching in their formality.

"The Hermenautic Circle." "Snake Handlers: Athens, Alabama." "The Bassanda Society of Talpa, New Mexico." Every photograph is the record of some mysterious enthusiasm and the people who shared it.

"I've never heard of anybody collecting weird societies before," Eve says, peering at these somber, long-forgotten faces. The light here is low; fortunately, the overheads don't point toward this corner of the loft.

"When I was a kid my mom loved going to yard sales, so it gave me something to do. Since they took themselves so seriously, I figure they deserve to have somebody else take them seriously too. I love that I've become the keeper of all these bizarre flames."

I love it too, Eve thinks. I am skirting the danger zone.

He undoes the buttons of her blouse, then turns to pour oil in the bath and takes off his own clothes facing away from her, allowing her to undress unwatched. She's grateful for his delicacy.

The feet of the bathtub are lion's claws. Fat-lipped dolphins—which Eve remembers from the lampposts in Paris—are painted around the outside. The faucet rises above the center. As Eve steps into the tub, Micajah lights three candles which sit on a rickety table. He settles at the end opposite Eve, his legs on either side of hers, his feet snugged against her hips.

What will I do with my feet? she thinks in a panic, her knees still bent, feet flat on the bottom of the tub. If she stretches out her legs, her feet will end up in a place way beyond her comfort zone. Resting her feet outside his legs would be even worse.

Micajah reads the confusion on her face. His laugh begins barely a second before hers.

"Give me a foot," he says, holding out his hands. "Leave the other one where it is, so you don't slip down."

Micajah rubs the arch of her foot, gently pulls each toe until it cracks, and then makes tiny circles with both thumbs at the corners of the nail of her big toe. Eve feels like a snake whose dry husk is dropping away.

She lets her left foot slide forward and edges it beneath him, so that it's pressed between the hard enamel of the bath and the firm muscle of his thigh. She glances down at her breasts, buoyed up by the water. They look as they did twenty years ago.

"Yann," Micajah says. "You haven't asked me about him yet. But I know you haven't forgotten. He wasn't just an excuse."

"I wouldn't have called you otherwise," Eve says.

"So you only want me for my contacts?"

Yes. No. She can't answer him.

"That's all right," he adds. "Any reason will do."

"Why do you want me?" She's horrified at having said it. She's always looked down on clingy women who need reassurance, women who ask their men, Do you love me? It's either weakness or feminine wile.

"You mean, why would I desire a woman twenty years older than me?"

"Yes," she says, relieved that he's taking her question at face value.

"It's a fair question. Funny, isn't it, how hatred and cynicism are this cosmic tide, and love is flickering and dim and needs a pilot light."

He places her foot against his abdomen, and holds it against him with his palm.

"First of all, because you don't need me. In fact, you really don't need me, I'm probably the last thing you need. You weren't looking for me, or anyone like me. You don't want to marry me and have my babies and play out some fantasy that's got nothing to do with me but everything to do with your buttons, your story. You're not looking for forever, and I don't believe in forever. I believe in now. And right now, this incredible woman, whose body and heart have gone through experiences of meaning so huge that I could never even imagine what it feels like, this woman whose grace sparks music in me and whose mind intrigues me and who is, by the way, really good-looking, is sitting in my bathtub, and I am massaging her feet. So, basically, that's it: instead of playing some fake role in someone else's story, I get to play a much more fun role, that's actually me, in a story you and I are making up as we go along."

He kisses her toes, each one in turn, and lowers that foot beneath the water, to rest between his legs. As he gentles her left foot out from beneath his thigh and lifts it out of the water, she moves her right big toe against him, feeling the blood rise and change the shape of his body.

The ease of it all, the absence of game plan, is new to Eve. Larry, and the few boys she knew before him, all made their circuit of first base, second, third, and home with no deviation. The unaccustomed frankness of the pleasure Micajah takes, and gives, makes Eve more daring. This, she realizes, is what being turned on feels like.

She strokes the arch of her foot against him, up and down. Momentarily, Micajah closes his eyes and a sound comes from deep in his throat, so low that Eve barely hears it. Then he opens his eyes and smiles at her. It's seductive, his absence of urgency. Maybe this is Tantra—that arcane, illicit practice Eve has heard of but never understood.

"I've known Yann for probably eight or nine years." His answer is as natural as if she'd just asked the question. "A friend of my parents introduced us. Her name is Barbara—you'd like her. When I went from being a sulky kid with a guitar to someone who could actually be considered a musician—though not a very good one—she thought that if music didn't happen for me, building instruments might be a good career move. I wasn't what you'd call academic."

"You worked for him?"

"Only sweeping floors and washing his dogs. I was still a teenager, an amateur, and you already know that Yann doesn't have a lot of time for amateurs. I was super lucky that he tolerated having me around."

"Because you learned a lot?"

"I learned a bit. The big result was that he got used to me. So when I asked him if I could be his apprentice—which I did, finally, yesterday—he said yes. Which is the first time he's said that to anyone. So I'm pretty stoked."

"You're not too busy with the whole rock star thing?" Eve feels rather silly saying that.

"Partly it's to stop me being too busy with the whole rock star thing," Micajah says. "At least, that's why I want to start now, not wait. If the whole rock star thing was all I was doing, God help me. I'd be either dead or so obnoxious I wouldn't want to live. If I ever got the moment of clarity to know it," he adds. Eve is coming to recognize Micajah's afterthoughts and non sequiturs as a way he has of measuring his words against some yardstick of truth, and shaping the statement more exactly if he finds it wanting.

"The work will keep me honest," he says.

When Eve wakes in the morning, she's alone in Micajah's bed. She sits up and sees him in the kitchen area making coffee. His bare back is bent to the side as he presses the coffeemaker down. Something looks odd . . . then Eve remembers he's left-handed. She's seeing his movements as if in a mirror.

"Cream? Sugar?" he calls. There is a mirror on the wall in front of him, in which his movements look more normal. An odd place for one. Eve wonders if it was his idea, or an ex-girlfriend's, to put it there, to allow him to see the bed as he makes coffee.

"Milk, if you've got some."

"Yup." He opens the fridge, pours milk into a pan. Eve hears the hiss of a steamer.

When he emerges from behind the kitchen counter, holding two big mugs, she sees that he is naked. Her reflex is to avert her eyes as he walks toward her, but his ease overrides it. It's like watching a cat move. Lean as he is, she can see the V-shaped muscles of his abdomen tensing as he walks.

The previous night, when they got out of the bath, Micajah wrapped her in a thick towel and dried her—just as she had dried Allan when he was six years old, delighting in the feel of his little body beneath the towel. As they ate their Chinese food, a pink neon sign outside the window blinked on.

"I'll give you a ride to the train station if you want to go home," he said. "But really, I'm hoping you want to stay."

A sequence of steps: the phone call, the mushroom, the Vespa, the clang of the door, the moment of darkness, the bath. With each step she took, Eve feared that the trail of breadcrumbs she was trying, mentally, to lay behind her would disappear, stranding her in a forest of dark, uncharted emotions. Still, she has already resigned herself to heartbreak.

It's the destination that's the risk. The reward is in the marvels of the journey.

She looked away from Micajah, her eyes falling on the vertical rows of somber-faced mystics and falconers and builders of ships in bottles staring out at her through the cameras of long ago. They are her allies. She has their benediction.

"I do," she said.

The sheets were fresh, still creased in straight lines from the packaging. So Micajah had planned to bring her back here, long before she agreed to come. Should she feel manipulated? She didn't. The heart defines the meaning, and Eve decided it was her choice what to see. As she inhaled the papery smell and felt the crisp cotton against her back, she was pleased that he had bought new sheets for her.

"I love these," he said, tracing the stretch marks on either side of her belly. "They look like a panther's claws."

Eve hated those marks. After Allan was born, she never wore a bikini again. When Micajah suggested the bath, she worried that he'd be repelled by them, but the bathwater and the candlelight disguised them. Overwhelmed by her decision to stay, she'd forgotten about them after that.

"I always thought they were ugly," she said.

"They're beautiful," he said. "They're your battle story."

He made love to her with deliberation, moving inside her with a hypnotic rhythm as slow as the pulse she'd sensed beneath her fingers. When climax came, she felt like he'd launched her off a cliff and she was flying. After a second, or ten seconds, or longer, she reached back for him, and he leapt toward her, the two of them holding each other in a tight, perfect unit, until gravity reasserted itself, they drifted back to earth, and Micajah settled himself on the bed beside her.

"I feel strange telling you this," she said, after a while. "It was four years. Before . . . before I met you. I thought maybe I'd never have sex again. Or even want to."

"That's obscene," he said. Then, "What kind of man neglects a woman like you?"

Micajah hands her the mug of coffee without ceremony, as if this is an ordinary situation. Could it be? Could this become normal for them? How soon would the shine fade?

The only way the shine will not fade is if this is the last time. And if there is another, that too must be the last time. Eve knows she must be rigorous. There is no future.

"You know the G-spot," he says, taking a sip of his coffee.

"Yes," Eve says warily. She drops her eyes to her own mug and sees that her hand is trembling.

"Actually, no," she says, "not personally."

She didn't intend to be so open, but she feels safe: he won't take her inexperience as a problem, or a failing. In the past, she turned her naivety into a source of pride. Now it gives edge to the adventure.

"You never tried to find it? Even alone?"

"I was never a hundred percent sure I had found it." She's unwilling to reveal that she made very few attempts. Pleasuring herself, she'd always felt self-conscious, even at the moment of climax. It wasn't puritanical shame; she just felt that she wasn't very good at it, and that her hand was a feeble substitute for a man. Her husband.

Or a lover.

"I read somewhere that it's only a theory," she adds. "That scientists haven't been able to find it either. At least, not consistently."

"That's scientists for you."

She laughs. "My husband was a scientist by training. Before he took an office job."

"Bang," he says, setting down his coffee mug with one hand while sliding the other down her breastbone, moving the sheets away.

"How about we try to prove it."

"Some theories can't be proven," Eve says. His fingers on her skin are as light as a ladybug. Her breath comes faster.

"Like gravity," she adds.

"Damn. So we may have to keep repeating the experiment."

"We could be accused of a lack of scientific rigor," she says. "This isn't double-blind."

The gold flecks in his eyes spark through the air between them and ground in the fibers of her body. He reaches over to a chest of drawers, pulls out two bandannas, and drops them on the bed.

"Your idea," he says. "Double-blind. You want to do it?"

Eve feels as raw as a newborn. It's not that the old Eve would have said no. The old Eve would never have been asked the question.

She folds both bandannas into blindfolds, places one across his eyes and ties it. He holds out his hands, palms up, for her to give him the other one. Before she does, she takes greedy minutes to consume him with her eyes: the strong lines of his cheekbones and jaw, the full curves of his mouth. She places her index fingers at the center of his upper lip, and strokes outward. He opens his lips, just slightly, as if obeying her command. She leans in to kiss him, her fingers on either side of his mouth where dimples would be.

The movements of his tongue and lips are almost imperceptible, yet the energy flow toward her makes her head tingle. It's like he's returning the kiss with his mind.

Eve puts the second bandanna in his hands and guides it into place, flattening her hair while he ties the knot. With vision blotted out, her other senses catch fire. She feels his breathing, soft as mist, against her skin, down her throat, brushing across her breasts. She hears the steady thump of his heart, distant sirens and motors, the cooing of pigeons on the windowsills, the creaks of the bed as he moves. His tongue plays circles in her navel, his strong hands stroking the insides of her thighs, gentling her legs apart.

Then, as his tongue abandons her navel, licking down the midline of her body, his fingers move north again, the sandpapery calluses etching arc after arc up her abdomen, like fireworks.

His strong lips kiss the tip of the cleft between her legs. His tongue, insistent, explores her. Every nerve in her body zooms in to those few square millimeters. She thinks, Maybe nobody has ever touched that exact spot before.

"That's not it." His voice is a low echo, barely more than a whisper. "I'm calling that the M spot."

At first, she doesn't know what he means. The conscious processing of her reason is sputtering, like a machine with its battery running out.

He moves down further, his tongue brushing against her clitoris. She gasps.

"That's yours. Found territory. I won't claim it."

The breath that makes his words plays across the folds of flesh, contours she's never seen. Under his fingers and tongue they take on unfamiliar shapes, rises and valleys that she never knew were hers.

His finger edges past the rim of bone to slip inside her.

"The I spot," he says. "Because I like it." She feels his tongue flick into her. "And because my name is Micajah, and I'll be your server today."

His tongue licks like a cat's around the very edge of the opening—though not quite all the way around—so that Eve can hardly tell whether it's still on the surface of her body or inside her.

"That's a C."

She forces her pleasure-saturated brain to do the math: he's less than halfway through his name.

His fingers again, moving inside her—his two index fingers, she thinks. One stays low, stroking lazy Cs on the bone. The other presses first here, then there, toward the sides of her body, the back. She hears a long, low moan, and realizes she made it.

"Aha," he says, "A. Good enough to come back to."

Without taking his fingers away, he kisses a spot on her inner thigh, just where the crease of her behind starts. Another spot that Eve has never felt specifically before, that's never been isolated and caressed.

"Is that J?" Her words are soft-edged and slow.

"If you like. Or it could just be a bonus, and this is J."

The two fingers are together now, kneading a hidden mound inside her. She wants to tangle her fingers in his thick hair, but the nerves that fire conscious action have been taken hostage. The entire network is devoted to only one purpose: to magnify the sensations created by Micajah's fingers, and Micajah's tongue.

"Back to A."

One finger moves, while the other continues to stroke on the mound he's christened J. Eve's whole body, not just her voice, has turned to honey. H for honey, she thinks, her brain firing lazily. H comes after G. That means the H spot is better.

"H."

She shudders against his hands, which are on her hips now, holding her tight against his firm mouth and his tongue as he simultaneously devours her and feeds her, sending wave after wave of energy flooding through her, fizzing like champagne at the crown of her head.

His mouth moves to hers, his breath merges with hers. She tastes the thick saltiness of her own pleasure on his tongue. This could all be a creation of her mind: his weight on top of her, the warm scent of his neck, the soft rasp of his stubble against her face. My desire made you, she thinks. She wraps her legs around him, pulling this creation of hers closer in, filling herself with him, cherishing him.

She feels his body taut as a bowstring pulled to breaking point, then release with a rush. The air around their joined bodies whirs with it.

"Micajah," she says, savoring his name, lifting the bandanna away from his eyes and then her own.

"The experiment failed," he says. "None of those spots was called G."

"Edison said he never failed. He just found ten thousand ways that didn't work."

"I could try changing my name to Greg. Though it's not long enough. Gregory."

"George," Eve says. "Still not long enough."

"Gogol. Guglielmo."

She laughs.

"Guggenheim," he says. "Peggy Guggenheim. If you swung that way."

He takes her right hand and guides it to the place he brushed over and left behind.

"Remember?" he says. "This is yours."

His index finger is above hers, its pad pressing on her fingernail, the two fingers stroking as one, in tight circles.

"E," he says. And with his third finger, he moves her third finger inside the bony ridge. "V." His fingers on hers are strong and precise. "E."

Again he spells her name with their locked fingers.

"E."

"V."

"E."

8

The air, through the open windows of the car, is damp and loamy. An infinite variety of green floods Eve's eyes. She's acutely aware that every in-breath she takes here, as they find their way on back roads into a forgotten rural pocket of Long Island, is the out-breath of plants. Micajah is driving; on the seat behind them is the instrument in its case, which they are taking to Yann. Micajah phoned; Yann agreed to look at it.

Eve is beginning to think of it as a talisman: beautiful and fragile, its gashed back like the gash of years between them.

The car is a 1990s Chevy Nova, in a dated shade of green. It's in good condition, but not what a car guy would call cherry. Certainly not pimped. Old rather than vintage. Entirely lacking in glamour. Not at all the car that Eve would have imagined Micajah buying with his new-fledged rock-star money.

He told her about it that morning as they lay in his bed, as now and then a diesel truck rumbled by on the Brooklyn street below. He was buying it, he said, because when he becomes Yann's apprentice he can't carry instruments and tools back and forth on a Vespa.

He's more excited about this, Eve senses, than about becoming a rock star. Talent and teenage dreams have brought him there, but she's coming to see that, in fact, he's dreading it.

"Want to come get the car with me? We can go exploring."

We again.

She felt stained by that look from the trainee survivalist. What are you doing with him? it said. Cougar. She dreaded being stabbed again by the judgment of strangers.

"I have to get home," she said apologetically. "I'm on a deadline. The planting diagram for a new courthouse complex."

The presentation was actually nearly three weeks away, but her words weren't entirely a lie. Eve makes deadlines for every stage of the bid process; a design deadline allows time for budgeting.

"How about next weekend? We can take the instrument to Yann."

"Promise he won't swear at me again."

"Promise."

She smiles. He's forgiven.

"He lives on Long Island, near my friend Barbara's house. We can stay the night with her."

In a shared room, obviously. Publicly, a couple. *We.*

Her chest constricts. She forces herself to breathe.

"Since we're driving, I'll come pick you up."

"It's in the opposite direction," she said.

"So what?" he said. "It's my new car. It needs some miles on it."

She gave him her address unwillingly, afraid that his mysterious sheen might be tarnished by her mundane New Jersey world. Still, she didn't want to make a drama out of arranging to meet him somewhere else. So when he called to let her know that he hadn't been able to collect the car yet and wouldn't be picking her up, she felt a tidal wave of gratitude to whoever or whatever had thrown his plan out of whack.

"What happened?" she asked. "I thought you were going to get it right after I left."

"I couldn't," he said, taking care with his words. "Something came up. An emergency. It took a while."

Obviously, he didn't want to tell her what had happened, nor did he want to lie. Eve is not someone who asks questions, who prods and probes. What they have is delicate. It needs protecting.

"Is everyone okay?"

"Yeah," he said. "It's over now."

She let his evasiveness rest.

She picked him up in her Ford SUV and they drove to an Irish neighborhood in Queens. Once he had his car, they'd convoy to a train station, where she would leave hers. She hoped he'd be quick, but he did a walk-around of the Nova, making sure there were no new nicks or scratches in the olive-green paintwork. She began to feel trapped, waiting behind the steering wheel, so she got out, but stayed near her car, feeling less exposed that way.

"You love it, right?" said Micajah to Eve, running a finger along the thin chrome trim. "You're jealous."

The seller, a middle-aged man in a loose T-shirt, scanned Eve up and down with doggy enthusiasm. His folded arms rested on an almost horizontal shelf of belly.

"Your son's a smart lad," he said. His voice had a natural boom to it. "Fine vehicle. Got another ten years in it, easy."

"She's not my mother," Micajah said quickly.

"What is she, then?" said the man. He's the kind of guy, Eve thought, who puts up his fists at the first sniff of a fight.

Micajah looked back at her. He'd have no shame in saying it, she knew. But he knew how tender she felt.

"I'm his lover," said Eve, staring the man down.

The man looked like he'd been punched in the stomach. Micajah turned his face away to hide his grin, and flattened the paperwork on the Nova's hood. Quickly, the man signed, took what was his, and disappeared back inside his house.

"That was awesome," Micajah said as he fetched his license plate and a screwdriver from a bag on the back seat of her car. "I never thought you'd say it."

"Me neither," Eve replied, and collapsed in laughter.

Micajah glanced at the man's house. "Do you think he's watching us?"

"I'm sure he is."

"Old guys like him," said Micajah, once he'd stopped laughing enough to speak, "they make their wives compete with younger women and they don't even know they're doing it. Well, guess what, my friend. You have to compete with guys like me."

As they drive east along Long Island in the Nova, the scene replays itself in Eve's mind. Micajah had been very quick, even angry, in telling the man that Eve wasn't his mother. She wonders about his mother. He's never mentioned her. She senses a wound there. Perhaps one day the subject will come up, and he will tell her what happened. She would like to know.

Micajah turns down a dirt lane, overhanging branches forming a leafy tunnel. It dead-ends at a clapboard farmhouse surrounded by ancient apple trees. Behind it is a barn, white paint weathered, weathervane on the roof ridge mangled by decades of winters.

In the open doorway, an enormous gray dog lies like a rug in the sun. Micajah bends down to stroke him.

"Hello, Seamus." He scratches the dog behind the ears. Seamus grunts and pants up at him. "This is Eve," he says, "she's with me."

Stepping between the dog's forepaws, he enters the barn. Eve follows.

A burly man with wild hair and a raveling sweater bends over a workbench, making tiny taps with a miniature mallet and chisel. He looks up from his work, nods to Micajah, barely glances at Eve, and returns to his focused concentration.

"Eve, this is Yann, the person I admire most in the world."

"That is only because he is young and does not know many people yet."

No "Hello," no "Nice to meet you." Yann's voice is deep and rough, almost a growl, with an indeterminate accent that might be Celtic, or Slavic. There's the hint of a lilt in it, as if this bearish man forms music inside him and releases it into the air as he exhales. Eve wonders if he might be autistic, or somewhere on the spectrum. His speech, despite its lilt, seems oddly careful. He barely glanced at her, directing his words to his tools; he didn't even smile at Micajah.

The barn is a treasure house. Its walls are hung with instruments, above ranged cabinets and shelves packed with books and also with animal bones and skulls. Feathers and flags hang on the uprights, along with old leather bags and pouches, strange objects of painted metal, long ropes and bundles of strings. The wood-plank floor is strewn with intricately patterned Persian rugs, faded and frayed. Ratty plaid blankets cover a sofa and two armchairs. A calico cat is curled in one, asleep in the warm shade.

Clerestory windows circle the room below the vaulted ceiling, overhung by the eaves of the roof, so that the light is diffused and even. Only the shaft of sun flooding through the open doorway casts a shadow: Eve and Micajah, inter-twined.

"Look, Mick. It came from Yemen, last week. A primitive tambur."

Micajah moves over to the workbench, his dark head close to Yann's matted gray hair. Their absorption is beautiful. Eve would rather watch them than have them make small talk for her sake.

She loves the smell of this room, a mixture of wax and sawdust and dog and the patch of wild mint outside the door. Her gaze drifts across the instruments on the walls: some barbarically rough, others diabolically complex, from three ropelike strings to what might be a hundred or more fine golden filaments. Some are strange hybrids: part guitar and part banjo, part keyboard and part string. She is fasci-nated by the giraffe-like necks, the round vegetable bellies, the strange protrusions and carvings that suggest fish and angels and monsters of myth. One, inlaid with ivory and mother-of-pearl, Scheherazade might have played; another, dark and fierce, might have driven dervishes whirling to their deaths.

When Yann straightens up, Micajah lifts Eve's case onto a table.

"We've brought you something."

Little crooning sounds come from Yann as he lifts the instrument free of the moth-eaten lining. She watches his fingers move across the wood, as if he is physically sensing the sound it would make. As he runs them along the back, he winces. It seems to take an effort of will for him to turn it over and see the damage with his eyes.

"I found it in a junk shop," Eve says. "I couldn't bear to leave it."

"Like the emergency services," says Yann, probing the edges of the gash. "Never give up, even after the patient is dead."

Eve's heart sinks. His tone is hard to interpret. It sounds closer to sarcasm than hope.

"Can you do something?" asks Micajah.

"That is a nonsense of a question, my boy. I can do many things. I can juggle. I can climb that tree out there. I can roast a lamb whole."

Micajah laughs. "Can you fix it?"

Gently, Yann lays the instrument along the sofa's edge, fitting its bridge and strings into the cavity between the frame and the cushions. His fingers slip inside the hollow. Then he buries his face in the gash, as if searching for a sign of life.

He doesn't seem to care, or even notice, that Eve's eyes are fixed on him. If only the force of her will could make him say yes, he can fix it, and yes, he will.

As if he finds it too hard to watch Yann's process of diagnosis, Micajah picks up a violin and softly starts playing. He holds it in a way Eve has never seen: not jammed under his chin but almost upside down, its end resting in the crook between his bicep and the curving muscle of his shoulder. His eyes lose focus, as if he's seeing only the music inside his head.

Eve recognizes the melody immediately. She's been trying to recapture it since that night when she first heard it, trying to haul its notes out of a dark well in her mind. She went to play it again right after she saw the words "For Eve" and felt the blood pound in her ears, but the link had vanished. She searched her computer and could find no sign that the message, or the file, had ever existed. In the weeks since, it has become as insubstantial as a dream.

The tune, as Micajah plays it now, has the feeling of a traveler following an intermittent light in the fog. Searching; hope; joy at the prospect of deliverance; loss; searching again. Music has never spoken to her so directly before, never conjured up such clear emotions. She relaxes, letting it take her on its journey. Yann will answer what he answers; she cannot influence him.

She feels Micajah look over at her and glances up from her drifting state. As their eyes meet, she sees a shadow come over him.

He stops mid-phrase and takes up a different instrument, something Eve can't name. He drops into a low chair and rests its base on his lap, the neck rising high above his head. He saws the bow roughly across the strings. The search is no longer a tender quest. It's desperate.

Yann's hands stop exploring the gash. He looks at Eve, accusingly. Whatever this torment is in Micajah's heart, Yann believes she is to blame.

When the melody ends, Micajah hangs the strange

instrument back on the wall and goes outside without looking at Eve. Yann puts a hand on her arm, not holding her back but telling her silently, firmly, not to go.

"You are the woman who called me," he says. "Wanting to sell this."

"Yes."

For a millisecond, Eve wonders if she should have lied. No—it would be pointless, even if she was a good liar, which she isn't. A lie would offend Yann far more than the truth.

"I should make you eat it instead."

Eve feels that she is being tested. No response comes to her, so she just waits for him to continue.

"You said a lot more on the telephone than you say now," he says. "Plans and intentions and prescriptions for what in your mind I must do. Are they there still?"

Eve takes a moment before she replies. She has not changed her mind about selling the instrument, but she is not as certain of it as she was.

"Yes," she says. "They're possibilities. Not a definite plan."

Yann nods approvingly.

"A plan is an absurdity. The future cannot be commanded like a square of soldiers."

Again, no reply comes to Eve. She's surprised to realize that's not a failing. The usual social requirement to bat the ball of conversation back over the net does not hold with Yann.

"Still, we must have possibilities. Without them we are dumb beasts. You have others now too."

I could give the instrument to Micajah. The thought jumps into Eve's mind, but she's unwilling to speak it aloud. It would be a hostage to fortune, a marker put down on a future she's been telling herself repeatedly is impossible. Does Yann want her to promise that?

"What are you?" he asks her, his stare hard.

Though Eve can't articulate his meaning to herself, he has driven deep into her uncertainties. The question exposes the hole at the center of her self, the place where purpose lies. Yann is the judge, she the accused, yet she has no words to be a witness in her own defense. Later, Micajah will tell her that this was how she earned Yann's respect: with her rooted, honest silence.

"You are not a musician," Yann says. She feels the chill dissipate.

"No." On this score, she has nothing to hide.

"I am not either."

For the first time, she sees him smile—not at her, but at Micajah, behind her. She hears him step across Seamus in the doorway.

"I will try," he says to Micajah and, glancingly, to Eve.

Eve expected to feel relief. The satisfaction of success. Gratitude. What she feels instead is something impersonal—like the gears of fate turning.

"How much do you charge?" Eve is tentative about bringing up the subject of money, but feels she must.

"Raising the dead is a miracle," Yann says. "Not a purchase."

The tangy smells of sedge and salt mingle with the scented steam rising from a mug of fresh thyme tea, which Eve cups in both hands, enjoying the heat soaking into her palms. A bowl of ripe figs sits on the table in front of her. The walls of Barbara's kitchen are a pale robin's-egg blue that merges with the sky; Eve imagines that on other days, when the clouds are low and misty, the room blurs into the ocean. The cabinets are made of weathered driftwood, which Barbara collected herself, she told Eve—the remains of wrecked whaling ships and fishing boats, whose sailor ghosts she talks to sometimes.

On the drive to Long Island, Micajah told Eve that he was half in love with Barbara. You'll see, he said; you will love her too. Eve fought off her jealousy, telling herself that if Barbara was a rival, he would not be bringing her there.

Barbara is beautiful, with loose silvery hair and a wide mouth, lines etched in her skin by years of sun and wind, emotion and thought and laughter. It's not jealousy Eve feels, but envy. This, she thinks, is who I want to be when I grow up.

"Falling in love! Such a ridiculous idea! Like falling into a pit with sharp stakes at the bottom. And what do you catch when you want someone to fall in love with you? A Heffalump."

Barbara sautés mushrooms while Micajah slices tomatoes, freshly picked from a small fenced garden, crowded with flowers and vegetables, to one side of the door.

"It took a while, but I finally learned to run away at top speed from any man who was falling in love with me," Barbara says. "Or me with him. Who wants to fall? So much better to climb into love."

She pulls a few silver-green leaves of sage from a pot on the windowsill and adds them to the pan.

"The great thing about being seventy-six is that you can aspire to a post-sexual state. Love everybody, but nobody in particular. The secret of happiness. But you have to earn it."

"With blood and tears?" Micajah asks.

"No, my dear boy. Just with time. By aging. By paying your dues. You must have loved deeply and truly, at least once. Without an agenda, and absolutely without a list of things that need fixing. Have you, Eve? I won't even ask Micajah, he's much too young."

"No. I haven't." She gave up wishing Larry was different not out of love, but out of fatigue.

"I hear women talk, and it's all about what's wrong with their men. Basically, they're remedial projects. Like a house. It's never done. Once you've changed the knobs on the kitchen cabinets, the roof is leaking and the plaster has to be patched. And by then you've fallen out of love with the bathroom. The problem is this absurd idea that we're supposed to be monogamous for a lifetime. We're not penguins! Or is it grebes. How old are you, Eve?"

"Forty-nine in September."

"Forty-eight," says Micajah almost simultaneously. Eve

and Barbara share a smile. He's young enough that a year matters.

"Really, you two are perfect," Barbara adds. "Take the normal arrangement: a fifty-year-old man and a twenty-eight-year-old woman, rotten with agendas. He wants the arm candy, the massage of his ego, the tight ass in his bed. She wants the status, the security, the dress, the money. But reverse it, and it's the ideal love affair. Neither of you wants to reproduce, and neither of you wants to settle down—I'm sure you have no desire to pick up another man's socks, Eve, so soon after being released from the socks of your husband."

As she places an iron trivet on the table and sets the pan of mushrooms on it, she asks Eve, "Do you believe in love at first sight?"

Eve thinks for a moment: back to meeting Larry, meeting Micajah.

"I'm not sure. Should I?"

"God, no!" says Barbara. "How can you love someone you don't know? That's just an endorphin release, like jogging. I loathe seeing people lit up like pinball machines and calling it love."

Eve watches Micajah mixing the salad. Is this love, this feeling I have for him? It does not overwhelm her, hijack her sense and her senses. She does not stare at the phone waiting for it to ring, as she did when she was young. Whole hours of the day go by during which she does not think of Micajah at all; she works, she cooks, she ferrets out items for Deborah's shop, all with a new, expansive ease. She does not have to think about Larry's dinner, Larry's laundry, Larry's opinions. She does not have to think about Micajah's either.

She'd thought it was impossible that loving Micajah could bring her happiness; she's been afraid of it, of him, even as the reckless moments took her. But during the course of the evening, without her quite noticing it, the fear quietly slips away.

"If I love a man, I love watching him eat," Barbara says, with a funny growl.

"That's the sound of everything Barbara loves rolled into one," says Micajah fondly. "Ocean air, oysters, and good-looking men."

He prompts her to tell her stories: the married handyman she slept with every Friday for two years, and how she danced naked for him wearing only a headdress of egret feathers left over from her Vassar cotillion; the husband who ignored her to chase skinny women.

"If he wanted anorexic," she says, "he shouldn't have married me."

As they clean up after dinner, the classical playlist streaming through Barbara's stereo kicks up a Strauss waltz. Micajah grabs a dishtowel to dry his hands and pulls Barbara to her feet. She is a better dancer than he is, but it doesn't matter. He whirls her around the kitchen, into the living room, and back again, spinning first one way and then the other so that

they don't get dizzy. The waltz speeds up, faster and faster;
they're laughing as they try not to bang into furniture and
door frames and walls.

Watching them, as the evening light filters through the
leaves outside, Eve imagines the love that Barbara described
as a tree that she can climb and lie cradled in its sheltering
branches. Micajah has grown a tree like that for Barbara.
Perhaps one will grow for the two of them.

She looks more closely at the objects Barbara has chosen
to keep, on tables and windowsills. She picks up a piece
of whale ivory cracked by the years, one end carved into
a rose.

"What does that look like to you, Eve?" Barbara asks as she
collapses into an armchair, breathless and glowing.

Eve laughs.

"A dildo, wouldn't you say?"

"Is that what it is?"

"I have no idea! But don't you wish it was? What a lovely
idea, that you could feel the work of your man's hands inside
you when he's away, or dead, and in those days you might
not have known the difference for years. Haven't you ever
wondered what all that scrimshaw was for?"

Eve laughs again. "Flowers are rare, though. Usually it's just
patterns. Like kids' drawings."

"Well," says Barbara with a shrug, "not everyone is a lover.
Or an artist."

Out on the deck of Barbara's house after dinner, in the deep indigo of late evening, Micajah drapes his long arms over Eve's shoulders, his hands crossed on her stomach, his fingers playing with her navel through the thin fabric of her dress. The railings are twined with jasmine, its blossoms opened to the night air. Eve breathes in the sweetness and leans back into Micajah. There's a strange glow in the distance, as if the earth is brighter than the sliver of moon. The glow undulates, in the familiar movement of waves.

"What's happening? I've never seen anything like it before."

"Bioluminescence. Tiny sea creatures that generate their own light. Nobody knows why it happens, that there's a sudden shoal like this."

He kisses her neck, then unwraps himself from around her. "Let's go swimming."

They descend the dog-leg stairs and follow the walkway through the dunes. The wood slats are still warm from the afternoon sun. The drifts of sand are softly gritty under Eve's bare feet. As they crest the last dune, they stop, entranced by the sight: a gleaming, otherworldly tide.

"It's incredible," she says in a whisper.

Not just the sight, but the luck of everything that has happened in the last month, bringing her here. She cannot tear her eyes away from the ocean: in her mind, she is

already swimming in this alchemical bath, feeling it trans-
form her.

She hears the soft drop of Micajah's clothes on the sand.

"Race you!"

He takes off at a run. Eve pulls off her clothes, runs a few
steps, then slows to a walk. Running will rob her of seconds
of drinking in this unfathomable beauty.

Micajah dives into the waves, leaving a swirling nebula
behind him. When his head breaks the surface, he gleams
like a science fiction creature. Far above him, the five bright
stars of Cassiopeia form a scrawled M in the sky.

Eve lets the lacy edge of the waves play over her feet,
savoring its first touch on her skin. Out in the deeper water,
Micajah sends up splashes of blue stars.

"Come on! Come in!"

Eve is hit by a dark pang of self-consciousness as she stands
there naked: her breasts lower than they used to be, her hips
wider, the flesh of her stomach slack. She sinks into the waves
and swims out to Micajah.

Luminescence plays along the contours of his face. He
twines around her, holding her close while he treads water.
The seawater makes their skin cling where it touches.

With the palm of his hand he pushes the water up between
her legs, again and again: the ocean, fucking her. She curls her
feet against his hips to hold herself steady and open herself to
the waves that Micajah is making for her. Glistening droplets
of water run over his broad shoulders and down his biceps.

The stars are a reflection of the glittering sea. The longer she gazes up at them, the more pinpricks she sees in the fabric of space.

She wraps her legs around Micajah's chest and slides down, moving against him. She leans in to kiss his beautiful mouth.

"Let's go in."

As she reaches the beach, he grabs her ankle and pulls himself on top of her, burying his face in her neck and letting the waves wash over them. She thinks of Burt Lancaster and Deborah Kerr on the Hawaiian sand: gray shapes in fake moonlight, the membranes of bathing suits keeping the censors happy. If this was the 1950s, Eve thinks, I would not have a young lover. I would not be swimming naked with him. I'd be living in black-and-white, scolded by censors, half alive.

She wants Micajah, wants to fuse with him, to not know where she stops and he begins. Her nipples flame as the tide sucks the sand from beneath her, sharp granules of pulverized coral and bones and shells. She wriggles away and runs up the beach to the shower that's rigged up on a slatted deck beside the wooden walkway. With the fresh water running through her hair, she waits for him.

His arms swing loosely from the horizontal frame of his shoulders as he climbs the sloping sand. This is the picture of him she will always remember: striding toward her, long and lean, otherworldly, silhouetted against the gleaming ocean.

She gives up the shower to him. As she dries herself with a towel from a covered shelf, she watches his magical skin wash away. He turns off the shower and folds her into his arms.

"You're making me wet again," she says.

"Good."

She feels him pressing against her, a thick vertical line against her belly. She reaches her arms around his narrow hips, her hands drifting up the insides of his thighs to find the smooth unfolded skin between his legs—so mysterious to a woman's fingers. She never touched Larry there.

"Eve." With each breath, he moans or says her name. His teeth pull gently at her ear. His tongue finds the divot behind the lobe.

Pleasure bends her fingers into claws. For a moment, she's afraid that she's hurt him, dug her nails into that tender place. But there's no pain in the sounds he's making. He reminds her of a cat purring. As lightly as she can, she scratches with two fingers of her left hand, in a rhythm syncopated to the rise and fall of his chest.

He leans his head back, tangles his fingers tight in her hair. His collarbones rise in ridges under his young skin. She buries her tongue in the hollow space between them.

Beside them is a chaise longue the width of a double bed. A tufted cushion is tied to it with lavish bows. They sink onto it. His skin glows a deep, dark gold against the paleness of her skin, whitened by the moonlight.

"Tie me down," he says, tugging at a bow, wrapping the ribbon around his wrist.

"You like that?"

"I don't know."

"You've never done it? Really?"

In Eve's mind, Micajah knows everything about sex.

"I'm not lying, Eve. I won't ever lie to you."

The suppressed fierceness in his voice sounds like a warning: don't ask questions to which you don't want to know the answers.

She leans over to tie the loose ribbons around his right wrist. Her breasts brush against his face. He pulls her nipple into his mouth and bites her, hard enough to sting.

"Is that good?"

Yes or no? Her nerves dance along the verge between pain and pleasure. Her nipples are rigid as iron.

"Yes."

Her fingers fumble, her concentration and coordination shot. He has let his arm go limp. All his energy is focused in the tireless, tormenting caresses of his mouth.

Finally, she manages to tie a bow that won't come undone. She turns to his left wrist. His mouth moves to her right breast.

The second bow is tied now. Eve runs her tongue up his inner arm and along the ridge at the front of his armpit, learning more closely the geography of his body. The moonlight throws a shadow into the hollow at the base of his throat. Her tongue found it; now her eyes mark its identity, as an explorer names the features of a new land.

 She draws a line of slow kisses down his smooth chest to the nipple. She bites it, sharply, the way he bit hers.

He moans, his body twisting like an eel's.

"Is that good?" she asks.

He doesn't answer.

A fine line of hair starts at his navel and leads down to the dark thatch with that startlingly naked shape rising hungrily from it. It seems almost a separate creature as she curves her hands around it, then her lips, moving the skin that clothes it up and down, learning with her tongue the conical shape of the tip, following the jagged seam of the vein underneath down to the base where, like a vein of ore, it disappears into the depths of his body.

She hovers over him, drawing out the moment between finding the perfect angle for him to penetrate her and the sensation of him rising up inside her. She feels the breeze shift, moving from the land to the sea, carrying the scent of jasmine.

She pulls at the ribbons, wanting to feel his hands on her skin. Yet when he does—holding the weight of her breasts, following the swell of her stomach, curving his palms onto the width of her hips—she feels too big, too soft, too old.

"Shh," he says, feeling her unspoken self-judgment pulling her away from him. "You're a queen. Not some skinny little princess. You contain multitudes."

He smiles at the bafflement on her face.

"You're generous," he says. "You're spacious."

She laughs. "A little too spacious." But the edge of her judgment is gone.

"No," he says. "Gloriously spacious. You stretch my heart."

9

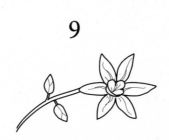

On the drive back to the city, Micajah speaks little. He did not say much on the drive out to Long Island either. She'd thought, being a musician and being young, that he'd have the stereo on, but he doesn't. Eve likes his lack of need to drown silence with sound.

She's not tempted to ask him what happened that day when he didn't go to pick up the car. She suspects that it threaded through the following days, when he didn't phone her, but he seemed at peace on their drive out, so she figured it was over. The sound of her song in Yann's barn told her that it wasn't over at all. The wail of the second instrument was the pain of new bruises on his heart.

Micajah's eyes gaze somewhere beyond the road ahead. Now and then, he half sings random words. Eve feels something like awe, sitting beside him as a song comes into being. She thinks of her own work as craft rather than creativity, and she holds it on a lower order than writing, painting, and music—the making of something out of nothing.

The silence from the car holds through the week. Micajah

told her that he'd be on a short tour with the band: distracted, demanded of, up all night and sleeping through the day. That he hates publicity, hates crowds, hates whoring for his music. That he probably won't be in touch because he'll be doing exactly that and he wants to keep her pure, in a clean corner of his mind. That was his word: pure.

She had a vision of his mind as being like those paper plates with ridges that keep the potatoes and the salad pristine, unsullied by the juices of the meat. She shares Micajah's fear of what they have being contaminated, but though she wants to keep him out of her world, she cannot segregate him in her mind. All thoughts lead to him, now, or detour past him on their way somewhere else.

She will not call him. Her mother taught her the rules—but even though those days are supposedly gone, she doesn't want to feel like she's chasing him. She wonders whether, in those early days when he texted and messaged and emailed and she was the silent one, he felt this frustrated longing. Surely not: he barely knew her. She had not blasted him open. She had not carried him up into the pink sky. Terrestrial life, day after day, with no idea when she will see him again, is leaden and dull.

In bed she pleasures herself, thinking of him. But it feels like a violation, as if she's using him without consent, like a date rapist screwing a girl drugged with Rohypnol. The idea of using a vibrator used to strike her as unnatural, even sinful, but now she goes online (having learned how to disable her browser's tracking feature) and finds, among the obscenely pink and engorged pretend penises, a sleek, lipstick-shaped object, small and discreet, designed to stimulate a single spot. She works her way around to thinking of it as similar to tweezers, a tool that most women own but don't discuss.

It doesn't make her feel self-sufficient, as she'd hoped. Instead of a man, she has a device. Orgasm leaves her drained rather than nourished.

She thinks often about whether she loves Micajah, whether she is in love with him, and what the difference is. He keeps surprising her with some new angle to love him for; yet how much of it is her own desire to be in love, since that's how these stories go? Like all little girls, she grew up into the creed that love is what we live for.

She feels a glow when she thinks of him, and not an hour passes now that she doesn't. Her body yearns for the satiated fullness of engulfing him as he holds her in his arms. But she can live without him. She can imagine being happy without him. What she cannot imagine is ever being in love, in the way she used to believe in love, again.

When she was young, being in love meant all or nothing, bliss or misery—more misery, now that she looks back on it, because the bliss was shot through with both fear of loss and a gnawing hunger that even the man she loved could never really satisfy. Something he said would flood her with joy, but most things he said were in some way disappointing. One caress would transport her; the rest of the time, his caresses fell obscurely short.

It wasn't Larry's fault, she thinks. I told him I loved him, and he believed me. It was my fault that I didn't know I wanted more. He wanted more too. He just realized it before I did. A sad, protective tenderness for Larry seeps through Eve, dissolving the contempt she feels when she pokes about in the wound that his departure left behind. His pursuit of happiness is like the halting run of a polio survivor: clumsy and jagged, but the best he can do.

She remembers a morning when she was alone in the kitchen. It was a weekend, Saturday or Sunday, she can't remember. Larry had already begun meditating in the mornings. At first, Eve had felt hurt that he did not come down to breakfast with her but disappeared into the guest room, to his altar. They were still sleeping together then, in the same bed and in the other sense, too. It was cold, a winter morning, and she made oatmeal. She warmed up some frozen blueberries in the microwave and added them, with real maple syrup. She felt a rare rush of happiness as she poured it. Its liquid sweetness would suffuse her, make everything all right. She served the oatmeal in a porcelain bowl and her spoon rang on it as she ate, its bell-like vibration hanging in the air.

She heard Larry on the stairs. He would probably want some too.

He went straight to the cabinet, not looking at her. Eve felt relieved that he was getting his own breakfast, and guilty that she felt that way. She heard a drawer open and close behind her. She hoped his silence was companionable. There were more silences than there used to be, particularly in the mornings, which Eve ascribed to the meditating. Wolves did not waste words, shoot off their mouths, make empty conversation. They did what needed to be done, looked after their own, were loyal to their pack but guarded a fierce independence of spirit. This new confidence and determination would be good for Larry.

Clang! Larry banged a spoon, hard, against a bowl, an inch from her ear. Eve jumped in her chair as if she'd been hit. He banged it again. The echo bounced around in her head.

Larry put the bowl back in the cabinet and the spoon back in the drawer, then walked out of the room and out of the house. He'd been mean to Eve before, but she'd always found a reason to excuse him. This time there was none. Her upset roiled with the injustice of it. The sounds of her breakfast had evidently disturbed his meditation, but wasn't the point of meditating to develop calmness?

For weeks, Eve fantasized about doing the same thing to him. A bowl in her left hand, spoon in her right, she would creep into the guest room, where he lay dreaming of his pack and the Arctic tundra, or wherever the hell wolves live. She would hold the bowl so close to his ear that the tiny hairs touched it, and bang it with the spoon. Day after day, the imaginary bowl shattered in her hand—a thing of beauty broken in anger. But her anger didn't subside. The fantasy meltdown was intoxicating, and her addiction to it made her feel that she was going mad. Now, looking back, she sees her rage as a sign of strength.

"Where the hell have you been?"

Eve hasn't seen Deborah for a few weeks. First, she was spending her weekends with Micajah rather than hunting out treasures. Since he's disappeared, she hasn't had the heart.

"I'm sorry, Deborah. I've just been busy."

"Bullshit! Come on, honey, Deborah knows."

Telling Deborah about Micajah would be equivalent to trussing him up like a pig with an apple in his mouth and presenting him on a silver salver for Deborah's delectation. She can imagine Deborah prodding at him to test the delicacy of his flesh, measuring the length of his eyelashes—and not just his eyelashes.

"We've got to find you a lover."

"I don't need to find a lover." That at least is technically true. "I'm fine by myself."

"Eve, you slut! What kind of vibrator did you get? God knows, the day I discovered vibrators was the day I broke out of prison, yelling for joy."

"Oh, Deborah, you know me. That's not it."

Though there's a turbocharge in holding the secret, she

longs to feel Micajah's name on her lips, to call up the image of him—and by telling the story to see on Deborah's astounded face the reflection of her own transformation. I have a lover, she wants to say. I *am* a lover—his lover— whatever that means. We're making our own meaning for it as we go.

On the other end of the phone, Deborah deflates theatrically, as if Eve has disappointed her by being the sexually timid woman that Deborah imagines her to be. In fact, she's not disappointed at all: she relishes the role of provocateur. She's the bold one blazing the sex trail. She'd be thoroughly confused if she knew that Eve had done things that she herself could barely imagine.

"Well, then, for Chrissake, Eve, stop sitting at home like Our Lady of the Thousand Sorrows."

Eve is not one for bars, but Deborah's favored hangout is not that kind of bar. No television screens, no sports pennants, no photos of cars. There's a hint of nightclub, but no sleaze or danger. It's decorated with photos of old-time movie stars "at home," chosen for maximum fakery. The spouses and children look like rent-a-families; every living room holds an unplayed grand piano, every adult holds a cocktail. The artificiality is both festive and comforting. Even glamorous people have ordinary lives, and even glamorous people's ordinary lives aren't quite good enough. And if glamorous people can act normal for the photographer, normal people can act glamorous for the camera-phone, with the help of soft lighting and hazy mirrors which let you catch sight of yourself among the stars.

"The girls," as Deborah calls them, are all in their forties and mostly still married. They are not on the prowl. Which is a good thing, as—other than the hot young bartenders—all the men there are the guarantor halves of stalwart married couples. Most of the tables are occupied by groups of women—actually, groups of handbags, since there's a dance space where the tables have been pushed back. The women take turns to sit out the song, drink wine, and mind the money.

The music is mac-and-cheese pop and throwback disco, too loud for talking. Normally, Eve would dislike that, but tonight it suits her. She doesn't want to trash Larry, which is what would be expected of her. She doesn't want to discuss Larry at all. Nor does she want to hear complaints about the other husbands, which vary only in detail from the complaints she used to stifle in herself.

In Deborah's eyes, husbands are a universally sad species. She doesn't respect them—and by extension, wives. Since Deborah's divorce, Eve has felt a constant undercurrent of condescension toward those who have stayed married and settled for what is by Deborah's definition the pathetic comfort of second-best. Now that Eve is single—in effect, if not in law—Deborah looks at her with a celebratory glint, as if she won't be satisfied until she sees Eve dancing on a table.

"Come on, chica! Shake that booty!"

Deborah drags Eve out to dance, moving backward, grooving to the beat. Only once they're surrounded by moving bodies does she let go of Eve's arm, shimmying her hips, lips pouting, eyelids lowered, breaking into a grin and then slapping on the sexy mask again as she sings along:

"You can ring my be—e—ell, ring my bell!"

Eve shimmies her shoulders, goading Deborah back. All around them, pairs and trios of women are bumping and grinding, exaggerating the sexy, pretending they're aiming it at one another. It's a playground with safety features built in: they're all straight, at least officially. Actual sex is not on the menu. A few of the women throw glances at the bartenders, just to see if they're watching, but the bartenders' smiles are just an extra spice.

Deborah rolls her hands one around the other in the classic Travolta move and flings a fist diagonally into the air. Suddenly all the women are doing it in unison: fist pump, fist pump, fist pump. Eve feels the energy rush surrounding her—the women laughing, flirting, teasing, with no male gaze to find fault with their aging flesh, no jaded man to please, no fear of rejection or threat of asserted control. Just bodies generating endorphins to lock into the pleasure centers of the brain.

The song ends: Anita Ward gives way to Soft Cell. Sweating, laughing, Eve and Deborah go back to their table. There's someone new there: a husband. He's balding and paunchy, but his shirt is open one button too far, revealing sparse mouse-colored hairs. He's trying to look rakish.

His wife, a heavyset woman with red hair, looks embarrassed and helpless. To Deborah she mouths, "Sorry."

Deborah waves it off.

"Jealous, Henry? Afraid Judy is getting up to something she shouldn't be?"

"I was in the neighborhood. Figured you wouldn't mind if I joined my wife."

Behind him, one of the other women rolls her eyes to the ceiling. Eve flops down and guzzles water.

"You can thank me for getting that water," Judy says. "I saw you going for it out there."

"You're a sweetheart," Eve says, raising her glass to Judy. The other women do the same: a gesture of solidarity and sympathy and not-holding-her-husband-against-her.

"Check this out!" says Henry. He holds up his phone to show a photo of Eve dancing, cropped at the waist and knees. Ass only.

"I'm gonna post it on Facebook, and tag it with Larry's name! I got a great one of Dora, too, I'm gonna tag that 'Chuck.'"

He gives a shout of laughter, expecting that the women will laugh too. The sweat of sordid excitement beads his forehead.

"Henry, you are clueless," Deborah says. "Get out of here. And if I see those photos on Facebook, your ass is gonna hurt so bad you'll know it's Deborah come to get you."

"Dickhead," she says as he leaves. "Sorry, Judy."

"It's okay," says Judy. "It's the truth."

"Your call," says Deborah, as Judy gathers up her bag to follow him out. "We love you, honey."

"Thanks," says Judy. "Love you too."

Eve's heart goes out to her. She knows what it feels like to make excuses for her man, to dredge up some level of respect when contempt threatens to swamp it. Henry, getting it so wrong, has made it clear for her: if Larry ever owned her ass or any other part of her, or thought he did—or if anyone else, like Henry, thought he did—he doesn't anymore.

Never again, she thinks. Never again.

A few mornings later, Eve wakes up with her lower back frozen. She heaves herself from lying to sitting and can't help yelping. It's as well that Micajah has disappeared. She would not want him to see her like this: an old lady hobbling to the bathroom, her body torqued, her face contorted by pain. The idea of having a lover at all, in this condition, is ludicrous.

Does she have one anymore? She's forced herself to get used to the idea that she may not. It's okay, she's decided, unwilling to let herself sink into drama. I'm one of the lucky ones. I got to ride the whirlwind.

Maybe this is menopause, she thinks. Four months ago was the first time she skipped. Born-again virgin that she

was then, she thought little of it other than vaguely registering the progress of time. Now it looks like she's skipping
again, and with Micajah she's been careless. Surely she can't
be pregnant at forty-eight? It is biologically possible. Could
the coincidence be this drastic: to lose a lover and lose her
bleeding all at once?

She buys a test on the way home from the gentlest yoga
class she could find, feeling the lurch of youth falling into age.
She pees on the strip of paper. Negative.

That evening she sits on the sofa with a heating pad pressed
to her back and a book in her hand. The words swim; her
mind wanders into thickets of contradictory desires. She turns
on the television, finds a series that's supposed to be good. But
all the actors are visibly acting, the plotline is overworked:
she feels like a Tourette's patient guffawing at a newsreader.
These actors rumble and scowl, swoon and sulk with a wary
eye to the next plot twist barreling into view. Still, the light
and the colors and the quick cuts are narcotic; this will get
her through until bedtime.

The drama ends; a talk show begins. Another actor: overly
casual, overly jovial, overly himself. And then, according to
formula, a band.

Micajah's band.

They're playing something discordant and post-apocalyp-
tic. The lead singer's feet are bare; long hair streams over the
shoulders of his elegantly cut suit. The spotlight is relentlessly
on him; Micajah stands to one side, edging always into the

shadows. There are two girls in the band: one is the drummer; the other, cute and pixie-ish, jumps around, her guitar and the lead singer's throwing riffs against each other like cage fighters.

The guitars collapse in exhaustion, but the song isn't over: a lone fiddle rises, like a soul taking flight from the bodies of the dead. The camera yaws—Eve senses the confusion in the control room—before finding Micajah. She imagines the cameraman, heavy equipment strapped to his body, the director yelling in his earpiece, closing in on Micajah like prey.

She flicks off the remote, unable to watch. She cannot imagine how he will survive in a world where the life forms that thrive have grown layers of artificial skin. Can he grow a skin like that, and grow it fast? If he does, the growing of it will consume him, and there won't be any of the Micajah she loves left.

She knows he fears it too.

The conference room of the town hall of Newton, New Jersey, is hot, the air conditioning grinding and clattering without much effect. As Eve turns a page on the flipchart displaying her planting proposal, she tries not to raise her arms too high, feeling sweat leaching through the cotton of her shirt.

The three men sitting around the scuffed table have

loosened their ties. The lone woman absent-mindedly messes with her bra strap, lifting it away from her skin.

"This planting scheme is based on ecological principles," she says. "Thrifty use of resources. A minimum amount of water. Which will, in the end, save money."

Her phone vibrates noisily on the hard surface of the table. It's a repeat notification. She ignored the first buzz as she was in the middle of the initial tour of her diagram. Now, she snatches a glance at her phone and sees the text—it's been visible for a full minute:

I want to fuck you

Her face flushes—and her body too. This is the first word from Micajah in over two weeks. Did any of the officials see it? The man sitting closest is grinning at her.

"Excuse me," she says, grabbing the phone and texting back:

In a mtg

She presses Send and drops the phone on her vacant chair. The chair is at the end of the table, out of sight.

"Sorry," she says. "This scheme requires a greater initial outlay, but I am conscious that these are taxpayer dollars we're spending." She flips another page. "As you see, benefits accrue in the long run."

One of the officials is now stabbing at his phone with uncoordinated middle-aged thumbs, as if Eve gave him the excuse. She's lost his attention; she hopes he's not a deciding vote.

"That's a pretty long run," another man says. "I'll be

running for reelection myself long before those benefits show up."

Damn, she didn't think of that.

Her phone vibrates again, the tweed upholstery deadening the noise. She drops her eyes to it:

Works for me

Eve feels a smile creeping over her face and banishes it. She needs this commission. The money Larry left her is running out fast. She turns to her next chart, which explains the substructure that would be installed beneath a surface layer of gravel.

Her phone wiggles on the chair. She snatches a glance:

How I hear you ask. With my fingers

"How?"

She looks up, startled. Who spoke? What was the question?

"I'm sorry," she says. "Could you repeat that? I want to be sure I answer you fully."

"Dogshit." The man at the far end of the table looks grumpy. "Sticks to the gravel. You deal with that, how?"

"Gravel is more hygienic than dirt," Eve says. "With this drainage layer beneath, it can be washed with a power hose."

"That sure saves water," says the woman.

"We're talking layers?" says the man nearest her. "The gravel's getting laid, you say? On a bed of something?"

Obviously he saw the text.

Another vibration:

With my tongue

Eve's pulse pounds in her ears. The officials are staring at her, waiting for an answer.

"It's called a French drain," she says. The nearest man splutters with laughter. Oh, God, she thinks, save me.

Calmly she explains that the water from the power hose is collected in a cistern and recycled by the drip irrigation system. Every other word is a double-entendre landmine waiting to explode.

As she flips over to the next chart, which details the comparative maintenance costs of traditional and xeric plantings, she hears another vibration. Her attention whips to the phone. Nothing. She imagined it.

Then, before she can focus back on the chart, the phone lights up:

With my cock

Followed immediately by: *Duh (That was you)*

"The xeric option requires more foreplay." Wait—what did she say? She meant to say "forethought." There's no sniggering, so maybe she did.

"Forethought," she says firmly. "Planning. Success is determined by the preparation. Once the planting is in, maintenance is minimal. I'll give you a moment to appreciate the savings year on year, as detailed in these diagrams."

As she waits for the questions to start, she can't stop herself looking down at her phone. All four texts are visible, three layers of ecstasy that could take her out of this dismal room with its tired cream walls and dead fluorescents. She's not going to get this commission; that's obvious. She edited out anything imaginative from her design weeks ago and focused her enthusiasm on the environmentally responsible option. Even that is too much of a stretch for them. They want something that's basically invisible. All she's doing now is going through the motions, out of some futile sense of pride.

"I'm not seeing any provision for training," says the grumpy man. "You're expecting old dogs to learn new tricks."

"Maybe the dogs could wash their own shit off the gravel," says the nearest man. "I think they call it golden rain."

The grumpy man gives him a withering look.

"Darren is referring to the groundskeepers," says the woman in a long-suffering tone. "I anticipate problems with the union if formal training in xeriscape maintenance isn't provided. By a certified expert in the field."

Which isn't Eve.

Another text:

With my heart

Eve feels her own heart being ground into dust. She needs clients, fast, but she feels incapable of signing them. Giving these committees what they want is not compromise: it's utter defeat. She's emerged from one living death only to find herself in another one.

She reaches for her phone, cocooning it in the breast pocket of her shirt while she flips the chart closed, snaps the stand into travel position, and collects her things.

"I apologize," she says. "It's an emergency, I have to leave.

Do please email me with any further questions. Thank you for your time."

The woman looks offended, even angry. The nearest man winks at her. The grumpy man looks satisfied, as if he's won. The man who was texting, who said nothing throughout, gives her a sidelong look which Eve takes as sympathetic. Perhaps, she thinks, he was texting with his lover too.

As she leaves the room, she feels the phone vibrate against her nipple. The thrill that rushes through her body makes her vision blur. At least the hallway is straight, with no obstacles. She dares not stop until she's made it outside.

She pulls out the phone, angles it to see the screen in the bright sunshine:

With my soul

When she reaches her car, she turns the air conditioning on full blast and pulls up the text screen.

That was mean, she types, and erases it.

Hello stranger, she types, and erases that too.

Why now, she types, and hits Send without leaving time for second thoughts.

She does not know if he's playing with her or if he's genuinely unable to stay distant any longer. The second, most likely, because she can't think him cruel. The blast of emotion she feels at hearing from him is not entirely pleasant. In this period of separation, she's started to feel the power of self-determination. The yank reminds her that Micajah, too, is a chain.

She sits there staring at the phone. The screen powers off, leaving it dead in her hand. Where has he gone? She feels irritation rising—at him, at the hide-and-seek of cybertalk. She considers calling him, decides against it. Even though he started the texting, the rules still apply. She does not need him.

She sets the phone down on the console between the seats and turns on the engine. As she's backing out of her parking space, she hears the ping. Changing gear, she looks down at it:

Are you free Thursday night? I will send a car for you

Despite herself, she texts back: *Yes*

10

The town car pulls up at Eve's house at sunset. Micajah's extravagant gesture makes Eve feel special. She sinks into the leather upholstery, notes the Evian bottles tucked into the seat-back pockets. Not once during the hour-long drive does she catch the dark-suited driver looking at her in the rear-view mirror. Well trained, or just uninterested? Would he be more interested if he knew I was going to meet my young lover? Eve wonders.

He had just got back to Brooklyn, Micajah said on the phone, and the band has to do this photo shoot, and it's a fucking drag, but maybe she'll find it comical, and he can't wait till tomorrow to see her, if she can come. She'd planned to work on her flower clock, but she said yes.

When they arrive, at a small abandoned dockyard on a desolate piece of shoreline, Eve isn't sure where to go. Purposeful twenty-somethings with iPads hurry past her as if she's not there. Then she spots the band: two girls, two other guys, and Micajah.

She has been craving the moment: his face reaching down

to hers, filling her whole field of vision; the crackling of their reflected gaze resolving into an all-encompassing kiss. Space and time contracting to the node of here and now, nobody but the two of them.

It does not happen as she imagined it. He smothers her in a hug so that she barely sees his eyes. He runs his hands over her face, and kisses her everywhere but on the mouth: along her hairline, on her closed eyelids, down her nose and on down the lines that run from her nose to the corners of her lips.

Her body softens to him; her mind does not. Why is he avoiding her eyes? She cannot fathom what he's thinking or feeling. He might as well be of another species or from another planet.

She buries her face in his neck, blotting out thought with the familiar smell of him, the tenderness of that private patch of skin.

It's public, way too public. Eve feels herself being assessed, judged, every year on her face and body counted. Why should she care? Micajah is diving into her presence as if into a warm lake.

The green of his eyes is her lake. But there's a chill in its waters she can't shake off: the distance his silence wrought, and something she can't quite identify that has grown in the dark.

"Okay, everybody, we're ready to go!"

Micajah opens a case on a folding table and takes out a fiddle. The band members stand in a loose group, corralled by the crew. The photographer is being strapped into a harness by two assistants. More assistants perch on ladders placed around the set.

Beyond the derelict docks, the seawater has receded, leaving mudflats. The skyscrapers of Midtown and downtown hover in the air, their lower reaches blocked out by rusty steel tanks. The effect is of bifocals: gaze up to the distant lights of the land of fun and money; rack focus and you're trapped in a decayed, threatening underworld. The lights of the skyscrapers reflect at an attenuated angle in the mudflats. The oily shimmer, like snail slime, must be why the photographer chose this location. It would be very hard to fake.

The briny, organic smell of the mud is more powerful than the stale fumes of the city. The breeze is on the hot side of warm. Eve's dress sticks to her lower back. The band members sweat under the lights. The bass player is stringy, with the look of an addict. He freaks Eve out a little: there's a stare in his eyes and he's drinking a Red Bull–coffee combo. The lead singer wears the same impeccable suit, T-shirt beneath, with bare feet and his own personal wind machine.

A stylist and a makeup artist buzz around the band, adding smudges of dirt to their faces, spritzing murky liquid onto Micajah's T-shirt to create a stain under his raised arm. The photographer wants hot, tired, sweaty from playing all night down at the docks. Maybe for nobody to hear but themselves.

"Can I rip this? Sylvain thinks ripped."

The stylist is holding the lead singer's T-shirt.

"Go ahead," he says.

She takes a scissors from her tool belt and makes a snip, then wiggles her fingers in and yanks hard. She looks up to Sylvain, where he's being hoisted into the air by cables attached to three cranes.

"Darling, you're the shit."

The stylist makes a few air scissor cuts in his direction, without looking at him. Eve feels as if the whole thing is an elaborate performance, or a game. It's crazy-making. And it hasn't even begun.

The bouncing-around girl—Bethany is her name—wears sheer black tights under minuscule denim cut-off shorts, a T-shirt falling off one shoulder, and high-wedged bovver boots. A streak of green in her hair frames one side of her face. Unlike the other girl, she wears no jewelry, has no tattoos.

"We're getting chemical poisoning out here," she grumbles. "Just Photoshop the skyline, motherfucker."

"You wanna know how many fucks I give about your weird-ass health shit?" says the other girl. "Zero."

Bethany's eyes are locked on Micajah. When he looks her way, she engrosses her attention in her hair, her makeup, her bootlaces, the other girl's clothes. She's in love with him, it's obvious, and equally obvious that Micajah is steering wide of her. They were together, Eve can see—but when? In these last weeks while they've been on tour?

I'm not his girlfriend, she reminds herself; we agreed that. He never promised he'd be faithful. Whatever Barbara said, we have only a short time together before I am too old for him, and maybe that time is up. And anyway, I thought it was over, and I was okay with that.

Still, there was a desperation in the way he held her when she arrived at the dockyard. What did that signify? He's focused on the photo shoot now, and looks at her rarely. When he does, his body relaxes, then tenses up again as he turns back to the task at hand. Bethany is his mirror, in negative: tensing when he relaxes, relaxing when he tenses. Eve pities her: the band is on the verge of making it big, and she wants the success more than she wants to heal her heart.

The only member of the band holding an instrument is Micajah. "Like a kid and his teddy bear," she overheard one of the crew say. It's clever marketing, implying that his relationship with his instrument is so symbiotic that he can't be separated from it. A guarantee of authenticity in the eye of the PR maelstrom. Seeing the image under construction makes burrs of doubt stick in Eve's mind. Real as she knows Micajah's passion for music to be, she sees the truth of it being sucked away until all that's left is a gust of air—one extra spin of the spin machine.

She wanders around the location: a generator powering the lights, wardrobe trailer, makeup trailer, an overweight journalist being fluffed by the PR team, a video crew recording it all. Eve feels invisible. She's used to that, as a woman nearing fifty—used to sales assistants in Home Depot not hearing her when she speaks to them, used to young women letting doors close in her face because they genuinely don't see her. Tonight, she's glad of her incognito. No one but Micajah and Bethany is aware that she's there.

She finds a table piled high with schizophrenic catering: Krispy Kreme, takeout pizza, salads of kale and quinoa, exotic fruits, bottled drinks with seeds floating in them and coolers of Pepsi and Red Bull. She picks up something called a Taos Mountain energy bar, full of strange-looking seeds.

"Sylvain has those flown in," says a young man in board shorts and a fishing vest, its pockets stuffed, pouring coffee from a Starbucks box. "He can't do a shoot without them." Eve imagines Sylvain like a champion racehorse, high-strung and skittish, groomed with expensive unguents in preparation for two minutes of glory.

"They're that good?" Eve asks.

"They're *amazing*." And even more so because they're flown in at Sylvain's demand. And Sylvain is amazing for knowing about them. If nobody else in New York is eating those energy bars, then nobody else in New York has what Sylvain has.

"Can I take one?"

The young man jolts visibly. Eve was just an excuse for him to show off his insider knowledge; he didn't expect her to put him on the spot. Rather than give her an answer that might be wrong, he scurries off toward Sylvain, who is being flown from ladder to ladder in his harness, shifting his camera's aim from one member of the band to another, clicking manically, yelling encouragement:

"Grr!"

"Aaahh!"

"More!"

"You play to stay alive!"

"Your music keeps the earth turning!"

As Sylvain shoots, Micajah plays snatches of song, seemingly oblivious. Is that an act too, Eve wonders, just building the image? The sinews of his bow arm flex, taut and strong like the steel cords holding up the bridge in the distance. Those hands and arms that have held her will soon be fantasized about by girls, women, men, who will never meet him.

He is both himself and not himself, and Eve cannot tell which one she is seeing. He puts his arm around Bethany, stretching the bow across her belly as if he's playing her. She leans back against him so far that he's holding her up. His other hand goes to the bone at the front of her hip, to steady her.

"I'm loving this, loving you!" Sylvain croons as the cables fly him close and hold him suspended above their heads—an oversized Cupid with a camera instead of an arrow.

One of the drivers ambles over to Eve and takes a couple of donuts. "You with the band?"

Eve laughs at the cliché. He laughs with her. He's friendlier than her driver was. Flirtatious, even.

"Kind of. With one of them, anyway."

"A mom?"

Eve knows that he meant only to ask whether she's a normal

person, not one of those media types who are working the shoot. What he really hopes is that she's a single mom, and that she wants to talk about her wonderful son or daughter, and that she will like him for listening.

"Not exactly."

She drifts off toward the parked town cars. He lets her go.

"Can you take me home?" Eve asks her driver when finally she locates him among the identically suited drivers and identical cars.

"Ready to call it a night, huh?" He's chattier already than he was on the entire trip here.

"I had a long day."

Her eyes closed against conversation, Eve feels the car negotiate the potholed asphalt of this derelict zone, stopping at each short block, edging gingerly around corners. Suddenly, there's a shriek of brakes and she's thrown forward. The hard edge of the seat belt slices into her neck.

"Goddamn it! What the fuck, asshole?"

She sees the driver glance in the rear-view mirror, worried that she'll complain about his unprofessional swearing.

"What happened? Are you okay?"

Her concern calms him.

"I'm sorry, ma'm. This guy on some piss-ant excuse for a motorbike just came out of nowhere and rammed me."

"Rammed you?"

"Straight up goddamn rammed me."

"Is he all right? He's probably drunk or something." Eve strains to see.

"Or something."

The driver pulls a handgun from the glove compartment.

"Stay in the car, ma'm. Bad neighborhood."

As he edges out of the car, Eve sees disturbance in the light in front of them: it bounces and flickers as something moves jerkily in the headlights. A figure stands awkwardly. Micajah.

"Oh, my God." Eve feels herself say the words rather than hearing them.

The driver advances slowly. Eve can see he's saying something. Micajah raises his hands, as if the whole thing is a joke. Then he wavers and falls to the ground.

Eve is on her knees beside him in an instant. There's a smear of blood down the side of his face. He smiles up at her. His pupils are pinpricks.

"You can't leave." His words slur. "You should kiss me."

"You're concussed," she says. "Your eyes."

"Yeah. Those are some bright lights." He closes them, as if he'll fall asleep right there in the road.

Eve turns to the driver, who has stashed the gun authoritatively in his belt—his walk-on part in the drama performed.

"He's one of the band guys?"

Eve nods. "I need you to help me."

She sees him thinking: I don't want blood all over my car.
"Please."

The driver snaps into action and hauls Micajah to his feet.
He groans as he puts weight on his left foot, his ankle giving
way. Later he will tell Eve that he stepped off the Vespa before
letting it crash into the town car. He didn't want to take the
impact on his wrists. Still, he risked a broken leg, a fractured
arm, to stop her from leaving. And all she was doing was
going home.

The driver shoves the Vespa into the gutter before closing
his door more loudly than necessary. Micajah winces, his
bleeding head laid back against the seat rim.

"What's your address?" she asks him. He tells her.

"Did you hear that, sir? In Brooklyn. That's where we're
going."

"Copy that." He taps it into his GPS. A map appears on the
dashboard screen. As she digs in the seat-back pockets for a
bottle of water, Eve strains to see it. She barely knew where
she was going that other, moonlit night. She didn't care. But
this night is edgy. She wants as much hard information as
possible.

She gives Micajah the water to drink, then takes the bottle
and wets the hem of her dress. It won't reach his face. She
eases him sideways and lays his head in her lap. As she dabs
at his temple, he squirms, pulls out his phone, and thumbs
out a text.

"Alex will get the bike picked up," he says. "If it's still

there. Probably won't be. Help some junkie get his fix tonight."

"Or save somebody who can't pay his rent."

"You live in a sweet world."

His beautiful face, laid in her lap, reminds her of a fallen angel, and a caged leopard. His eyes are the same hypnotic, depthless green as her cat's.

"That was a crazy thing to do."

"I didn't want you to go without me."

"I was tired. You were busy."

"Yeah. I was busy." His anger seems to be dropping away. "It was Bethany that saw you go."

Bethany, who is in love with him. One eye on Micajah, one eye on Eve, the whole night.

"She told you?"

"Nah. I just saw her chill out." And then, as if Eve needs explanation: "She's jealous."

"You don't have to tell me. I don't want to know."

He closes his eyes again and reaches one arm back over his head, behind Eve's waist. His fingers find the bones of her lower spine. He begins to massage them—more strongly than she'd have expected after the hit he just took. She thinks again of her cat, the way he closes his eyes and shuts down one level of consciousness but stays trigger-ready to pounce.

The town car pulls up in front of the distinctive steel door. Eve remembers the first time she came here: penetrating the building's post-industrial disguise, the labyrinth of concrete stair-stepped passages, the heavy doors that slid aside. She gets out and goes around to the other side to help Micajah.

"You want me to wait?" the driver asks.

She imagines sitting alone in the car being driven back to New Jersey. That feels safe, which is not what the thought of staying feels like. But if he has a concussion, he shouldn't sleep alone.

Before Eve can reply, Micajah says, "No. Go home." Then: "Thanks, man. Sorry if I dinged your car. Don't worry, the label will make it right."

Dozily he fishes out his keys and drops them in Eve's hand, lets her figure them out. Eve has the sense that he's faking it, to some degree. He leans on her as they climb the stairs, lets the wall support him as he waits for her to unlock his door.

The stalactites of photographs form, tonight, a maze of obsessions. Eve steers him to his bed, then goes to the kitchen. She finds peppermint tea bags but no kettle. She fills a sauce-pan and sets it to boil. In the mirror by the stove she sees him sitting up, a violin stretched out along his arm.

"Listen," he says. "This is yours."

He plays the melody she knows as well as her own heart-beat. His playing is sloppy, with a few bum notes and slurs where he seems to lose his focus. Eve sets down the tea mug and settles at the foot of the bed.

"Lover we'll surrender to the sweet smell of nature
Bewitched by the danger of its blossoming nectar . . ."

This is the first time she's heard the lyrics. He speaks them rather than singing them, roughly where they would go if they were sung. He stops after one verse.

"You like it?" His voice is slow, as if he's half-asleep, or hypnotized.

"Yes."

"Thanks for giving it to me," he says.

For a moment she wonders if he's being sarcastic, implying that she should have thanked him. No—he's sincere.

"Will you play it again, all the way through?"

"Will you listen again?"

"Yes."

"Then forget it."

"What do you mean?"

"There's different ways to hear. You can listen with your ears and your head, or you can take the music into your body." His smile is languid. "Like with a lover. Lose your rational mind."

Again she feels a sense of foreboding.

"Remember the roof?"

"Yes."

"If you fell, you'd have died."

"I know."

"And it was more intense than you could have imagined, right?"

"Yes."

"So." He reaches for his jeans, on the floor beside the bed, and pulls a small silver box from a pocket. Inside are pills.

"Let me give you a listening experience that will ransack

your mind." She's never taken LSD and doesn't want to. Bill went into that world and never came out.

"What is it?" If she was on her feet, she'd be backing away.

"Quaaludes."

Eve recognizes the word vaguely. She saw it in a newspaper, maybe, something her parents didn't want her to know about.

"Yeah," Micajah says, reading her thoughts. "Kind of retro." He moves his hand, holding the pill, toward her mouth. "They don't call them that anymore. Same shit, though. Same beautiful seduction."

"No."

He pulls his hand back as if she's slapped it. "I can call you a cab, if you want. No judgment."

No judgment, she repeats to herself. But if that was a concussion she saw in his eyes, this would be a very stupid thing to do. Still, she's pretty sure it wasn't. There's nothing dull about the workings of his mind.

It feels like a test—though it isn't Micajah who is testing her. It's not a power game or a dare; she trusts him that it's all in service to the music. This may be a great idea or a terrible one, some cosmic justice evening out her incredible, undeserved luck. If that's the case, a failure of nerve now would be an offense against destiny.

He brushes the corner of her mouth with the top knuckle of his index finger, back and forth, as if he's stroking her with a feather. His fingers touch her tongue as he places the pill on it. She's woozy already, her fear of the unknown shot through with excitement. He's taking me further and further, she thinks. And she has no idea where her boundary lies.

Micajah presses the back of his hand under her chin to close her mouth, and holds the tea mug to her lips. She feels the pill slide down her throat.

"Now take your clothes off, and get in the shower with me."

Micajah soaps her entire body: neck, shoulders, breasts, waist, stomach and back, her hips, thighs, calves, down to her feet. Every nerve ending is called to attention, one by one. A velvety euphoria steals over her.

"Are you there yet?" he asks as he wraps a towel around her. He rummages in his closet and finds a fleece shirt of faded dark plaid, softened by years of washings.

"I think so." Her voice sounds distant, as if it's coming across a lake, through fog.

"Put this on." He holds the shirt open for her. "I don't want you to be cold."

It reaches to her thighs. There are rips in places; air strokes her skin. Buttoning it is a huge task, so she pulls it around her like a coat.

He has put on some pajama-like trousers that wrap and tie around his hips. He props her up in his bed against a mound of pillows. He dims the lights almost to blackness.

"This time," he says, quoting the line, "it's for real."

Shafts of pink come through the slatted blinds from the sign across the street, striping his bare chest and his feet. As he plays the intro, he says, "It'll be Lowell's voice on the track, when you hear it. Great voice, Lowell. Almost as great as the hair." He grins. "Next to him, I sound like a frog. You can kiss me later."

Micajah's singing voice is quiet and deep, wavering on and off the melody. He does not take his eyes from hers. It's almost more than she can bear. She wants to scream, run, explode. Her limbs are so heavy that she is melting into the bed.

When he reaches the bridge, he closes his eyes. Eve's gaze lingers on the muscles of his chest and abdomen, contracting and loosening as he moves the bow across the strings, the music itself making patterns in the fibers of his body.

"I'll kiss across the borders of your once cold shoulders
When the night blooms jasmine . . ."

The music floods through Eve's veins, warming her then chilling her with a minor chord, as if her body is an instrument on which Micajah is playing a melody of shifting temperatures. She is made of thick liquid, mercury, quicksilver. She will never be caught again.

Micajah stretches the final note out to the borderline where sound meets silence. When she can hear it no longer, Eve opens her eyes and sees the vibration shimmering in the neon aura surrounding him.

"I want to write it on you," he says.

He slides his hands into the fleece shirt and places his palms flat on her belly, moving them apart as if he's smoothing out a piece of paper. The shirt opens.

"What?"

"Your song."

He sees her look of apprehension, and cups her face in his hands.

"Do you think I want to hurt you?"

"You're . . . different. You scare me." It's hard to find the words and put them together coherently. The various functions of her brain—those that know and choose words, those that connect words, those that form words into speech—are galaxies apart.

"It's just ink. No piercing. No sharp objects."

He writes with his fingernail across her ribcage, half-singing the words. "Lover we'll surrender . . ."

"Okay," she says, resistance evaporating at his touch.

She watches him as he swims out of focus and returns with a bottle of ink and a long-handled pen.

"You have it ready," she says.

"Nights when I just want to give up," he says, "I write out my songs. Make them look beautiful."

He dips the pen in the inkpot and draws a curved line underneath each breast, a flower where the two lines meet. He begins the words at the next rib down, pausing every few letters to dip the pen in the ink. As he moves the nib in slow curves, from left to right, she feels it rasp softly against her skin, like the touch of a worn-down cat's claw.

"Don't move," he says. "Hold it in. It's Tantra."

She steels herself against the tickle but, because of the drug, her muscles are as yielding as rubber. Yet her nerves are as tense as the rope in a tug o' war, stretched between surrender and control.

"Shh, Eve. Not yet. Breathe."

Her mind snatches at an instruction from yoga class. She opens her throat and inhales a deep, conscious breath. But she can't keep to it. Her fingers clutch at the sheet to try and stop herself moving under Micajah's relentless pen, swooping below her navel. Soon, she knows, she won't be able to hold it in any longer and her body will convulse, the line of ink will spiral in a craze of whirls across her body.

The pen moves lower. He writes what feels like a looping capital letter around her left hipbone, and moves in toward the center again.

"Almost there."

Eve's every breath is a moan now, a titanic struggle not to move. Micajah dips the pen in the ink bottle and returns it to her skin. Beneath the nib, she feels his initials, "MB," written into her in mirror writing. The lightness of the pen's touch makes her think of him signing a scrap of paper and releasing it to the wind.

Eve is adrift in a dense and trackless forest, fronds brushing her skin, somewhere between waking and sleep. Though her eyes are too heavy to open, she feels the darkness striped by shafts of light. Hybrid fishy creatures surround her. There is a narwhal, with a unicorn's horn.

She does not want to open her eyes. Sight will wrench her out of this floating, back into time. She's afraid that when the hallucinations shatter, their edges will be sharp.

The tip of the horn prods her side. The narwhal does not glow like a unicorn should; its white gleams sinister and dull. Eve wants to escape from it, but she cannot move. Her body, which was weightless in the dream, now feels leaden. The horn pushes into her, like someone testing a joint of meat in a roasting pan.

She feels it probing between her legs, searching for the spot to press that will make her moan. It wants a sound from her, she knows. She tries to hold the moan back, but she cannot: the pressure is too insistent.

A warning siren is wailing in Eve's brain, but faintly, as if she's hearing it across a vast distance. With a huge effort of will, she manages to open her eyes.

Looking down at her from above is a cold and curious face. She should recognize it. She tries to pull the scattered fragments of her brain back together, feeling like she's hauling on heavy ships' ropes.

Bethany. The girl from the band.

She is naked, thin as a bundle of kindling. Her body is the

dead white of the narwhal. In her hand is the long-handled pen. She's teasing Eve with the blunt end, as if probing a specimen for reflexes. Eve tries to move away from it, but her limbs lie useless. The only movements her body consents to make are those that Bethany is controlling.

No, Eve wants to scream at her renegade body, you obey me! But the quaalude has reduced her to a mechanism of stimulus and response. That Bethany could make her moan appalls her. That's the violation—not the physical prodding. In that moment, Bethany stole her soul.

And Micajah. Does he know Bethany is doing this? Where is he?

Her eyes skid to the bed beside her, where his golden body lies sprawled face down across the twisted sheets. Did Bethany kill him?

"Yeah, right," says Bethany. Then, contemptuously, "Drama queen."

Did she say it out loud? She thought that she just thought it. Eve's mental processor is working at a glacial pace. She focuses on Micajah's chest, sees its steady rise and fall. Why was she so terrified that he was dead?

Bethany is still probing at her with the hard end of the pen. Eve heaves herself away. Bethany jumps back as if from a spitting fire.

Lurching on her feet, aware that her escape is a spectator sport for Bethany, Eve tries to remember where, last night, she left her clothes. They're in a heap on the floor beside the shower. Eve pulls her dress over her head, slips into her sandals. Wrong order: she's forgotten her underwear. She stuffs it into her handbag and stumbles past the strings of forgotten societies toward the door.

Bethany, still naked, stands in front of it, barring Eve's exit. Her eyes drill into Eve's.

"Did you like it when he ate you?"

Eve keeps her face blank. By force of will, she will retake control. She will not let Bethany curdle the bliss of that morning with hate.

"I taught him how to do that."

Eve stares through her, to the door, to the world beyond.

"We used another girl to practice on."

If she falters, she'll be broken. She cannot let Bethany's words touch her. Her only weapon is patience. She will not ask Bethany to let her leave. Bethany's laughter would cut her like a flail.

A minute passes, two, five. Bethany reaches out a hand as if to a skittish animal. Eve holds herself rock still.

Bethany's hand moves to the hem of Eve's dress, lifts it. Eve feels the brush of the fabric rising up her thighs. Then Bethany's finger pushes into her body, curling and beckoning, like she's chucking a child under the chin.

She could resist. She could probably overpower Bethany's scrawny body, but any reaction would be Bethany's victory. Rage is smoldering inside her; she'll let it flame later. This is a battle of wills.

You cannot break me, she thinks, making the words ring loud in her ears. But you are snapping like a twig.

Bethany brings her hand to her mouth and sucks Eve's juices from her finger. Eve pulls her focus back and meets Bethany's icy stare head on. On Bethany's arm is a fresh red weal, where a cut has healed over. Seeing Eve see it, Bethany flinches.

With the speed of a snake striking, Bethany's mouth covers Eve's, pressing hard, like someone setting glue. She flicks her tongue over Eve's lips as she pulls away.

"Hit the wipe-my-butt highway, Eve," she says, unchaining her smile, stepping aside to unblock the door.

With her hand on the door latch, Eve takes a final look around the apartment: the big windows, with the pink neon fading into the pink sky of dawn; the musical instruments scattered haphazardly about; and Micajah, unconscious on the bed. There is a smear of blood on the sheet near his head, where the wound reopened.

11

Out on the street, Eve called the paramedics and showed them where to go before heading off to find the subway. She asked what hospital Micajah would be taken to, and phoned later that day to check on his condition. He was never admitted, they said. Evidently, the paramedics found nothing seriously wrong.

Was Bethany the contamination Micajah feared? She cannot believe that he had anything to do with her being there that night. He would not have shown Eve pleasure only to put it as a toy into Bethany's hands. However Bethany got there, the truth is that she, Eve, cannot function in Micajah's world. She is illiterate in reading its rules and the motives of the creatures in it. And she cannot bring him into hers. The interdimensional realm that popped up to cradle them is gone.

It's over, she tells herself. Never, for the rest of her life, will she feel that way again. And the torture of knowing that is the price she has to pay for it. She was, she knows, touched by fortune: Larry left, Micajah appeared, the tumblers of a kind fate fell into place. And now they've been set spinning again.

The worst anguish is watching that soaring passion shrivel into the past, settling into a niche in her memory, like a niche in a mortuary. She fights back obliquely, by trying to recall the pain of childbirth—the only experience in her life that matches up to the intensity of what she felt with Micajah. But she can't. Her memory is just a story, framed and tamed, something she knows she once felt: the rushing agony that barely ebbed before it shredded her again, the terror as the epidural needle punctured her spinal cord. It's hardly more potent than if it had happened to someone else.

Time will sand Micajah down, too, into a story that even she may one day not entirely believe.

She'd imagined their relationship would end in a slow fade—no drama, just graceful acceptance, the two of them wishing each other well. She never thought she'd have to wrench herself away from him. This feels violent, brutal, as if she's slowly strangling a helpless thing, pressing relentlessly until it stops kicking and the breath is gone.

She put Caller ID on her landline so she knows which calls not to answer. She ignored the barrage of texts and voicemails until it died away. The ink washed off her body, leaving faint stains. She thinks of them as a crash survivor's scars.

She feels as if she has no skin, no protective membrane around her. The amount of pain in the world is more than she can bear. At times, she longs for Micajah so much that it feels as if her heart is being dragged out of her chest. She's nauseous, can't eat; then can't stop eating, desperate to feel something other than empty. A constant headache rings the socket of her left eye. She thinks of it as the Micajah headache, blurring the sight of that eye and skewing her sense of perspective.

At night, half awake and shivering, she battles with the sheets, as if she's snared in a net on a stony northern beach. During the day, she's dim-witted and drowsy, nodding off at the wheel of her car, forgetting appointments, mangling the words for things. Sometimes she's seized by an urge to scream, and she has to dig her fingernails into her palms to suppress it. Most of the time she's deadened, all emotion wrung out of her.

All she's ever lost—Larry, her brother Bill—has become an amorphous mass called Micajah. Bill used to play Bowie on his stereo, and the songs haunt Eve, as if Bill's ghost is trying to communicate with her. Like Major Tom, she's lost the connection. Lost all her tethers. Even the umbilical tether is gone. Allan is in another orbit, living his own life. Close as they are, he only waves as he floats by.

This is what she was afraid of when she shut down after Bill's death and married safe, predictable Larry—that she would fling herself out too far.

She does not want to see friends, because she does not want to talk about Micajah, yet Micajah is all she wants to talk about. Talking about him will nail down their love affair as an objective fact. Her mind is tangled with him: all she knows of him, all she has thought about him, all she expects and suspects and rejects of him. But she is losing him a second time. Hour by hour the reality of what they had is disappearing, undermined and destabilized by the overwhelming presence of Bethany. Why was she there? Did he know she was coming? Is that why he gave me the quaalude?

I should find solace in work, Eve tells herself. But she can't muster enthusiasm for other people's gardens and civic plantings. Larry was right: her business was just a plaything. Anything that demands her full attention rips her mind away from its obsession. Anger rushes through the gash, like a bloody pulsing wound.

Her cell phone runs out of battery. She leaves it that way.

She finds it hard to get up in the morning, hard to make herself go to bed. One day she wakes at three in the afternoon, after dozing away most of the daylight hours, and pads downstairs to make coffee, try to function, get to her work. She glances out the window next to the front door and sees a familiar green Chevy Nova. Sitting on top of it, cross-legged, is Micajah.

She feels her insides leap into her throat, as if she's going to vomit. She shrinks away from the window. Why am I hiding? she thinks. This is my house. He is stalking me. I should call the police.

But then, she thinks, I would have to explain it. And I cannot even explain it to myself.

She moves to a shadowed spot where she can see through

the dining-room window without being seen from outside. Micajah is sitting just as he was before, gazing down the street rather than at the house. She wonders how long he has been there. All day? There are no lights on and the garage door is closed, so he cannot tell if she is home. She wonders if he rang the doorbell, and maybe she was so deeply asleep that she didn't hear it. That's hard to believe; the doorbell is loud and jangly, so that she can hear it even if she's at the far end of the backyard. No, he didn't ring.

She watches him, as resigned and quiet as someone sitting shiva by a deathbed, and understands that this is the last effort, the one that has to be made when all hope is lost. He is expecting nothing from it. This is his strange sense of rectitude, an old-fashioned belief that something truly important must be done in person. He must offer himself; she must reject—not a phone call or an email, but him. If he gets no response from her, whether because she is ignoring him or because she is not home, he will not be back.

He'll stay until nightfall, she guesses, correctly. Then he will go.

A week passes, then another. Debt collectors' letters are starting to arrive. She lets the envelopes pile up unopened. Driving, doing necessary errands, she zones out and finds herself in front of Allan's elementary school, or the dental clinic she used to go to, or the office that used to be Larry's.

Making her way home along streets made unfamiliar by new development, something catches her eye: a craft store.

An impulse seizes her. As she swerves her car across a lane of traffic into the parking lot, the driver behind honks angrily. To her own surprise, she's laughing.

When Eve finally recharges her phone, it pings crazily with texts and missed calls and voicemails. A few days pass before she builds up the courage to check them.

Eve, my dear. It's Barbara, Micajah's friend. I have something of yours. How do I get it to you?

Yann didn't say whether he'd repaired the instrument or abandoned the job, Barbara tells Eve when she returns the call. They make a date for Eve to collect it. Come soon, Barbara says.

The Long Island Expressway is a skating rink, flooded by the August rain. Eve peers through the windscreen, barely able to see even with the wipers going full blast, and pulls into a lay-by to wait out the storm. She tries to smother her hopes and stay realistic as she sits in her parked car, rain sheeting on the glass. Almost certainly, Yann has not touched it. Even if it could be restored, who knows what damage he saw in Micajah, for which he must surely have blamed her? It would bolster his judgment of her as a silly woman who picks up pretty things and disposes of them with no care for their souls.

In the aftermath of the storm, Barbara's house looks

windswept and lonely. Water drips from curls of peeling paint. Eve notices something she missed before: the cliff the house stands on is crumbling away. In a decade or two, the house will fall over the edge.

She knocks, but hears no reply. She tries the latch. The door is unlocked, so she enters.

The downstairs rooms are empty and cold, and there's a smell of damp wood where the windowframes leak. Barbara's spirit is everywhere: in the needlepoint cushions, the weathered silver driftwood holding shells in its hollows, the scrimshaw scattered on tables and windowsills. Eve smiles, remembering Barbara's bawdy joke and her wish that it was true.

She climbs the stairs and finds Barbara in bed, wrapped in a cardigan and a ragged cashmere shawl even though the room is hot. It has the sweet smell of sickness. Propped against pillows, Barbara is smaller than Eve remembered her. She looks frail.

"You should have told me not to come," Eve says. "Although, now that I'm here, at least I can look after you a bit."

"I'm fine. I don't need looking after. I have a dread of being nursed. Really, I'd rather die, I've lived long enough anyway. But thank you."

Barbara's eyes are still bright and her voice, though hoarse, has energy in it.

"Don't worry, this isn't the big one. Obituarists won't pursue you as the last person to see me alive."

Eve laughs. "Good."

"Toss the cat off that chair, and sit down and talk to me."

The cat mewls in protest and stalks away as Eve settles into a low armchair upholstered in faded blue velvet.

"I won't ask you what happened between you and our friend. It ought to be of interest only to the two of you. All things have a lifespan, so unless it was untimely murdered, we needn't mourn."

"It wasn't," Eve says. "The end was strange, and sudden. But I think you'd write it up as natural causes."

Barbara nods. "Micajah said the same. Though he took it as his fault. He felt he'd hurt you, which pained him."

"He did. But it's all right. It was always part of the deal." Eve is still struggling to make sense of that night—or, rather, struggling to make it not matter. "He didn't know that," she adds. "It was the deal I made with myself."

Barbara takes a drink from the mug beside her bed. "I do love that boy, battered angel that he is."

"Battered?"

"Has he not told you his story? It's his to tell, not mine. Perhaps one day when you are friends again, he will."

Eve shrugs. "Our lives are so different, we might as well live on separate planets."

"You met once. Why not again? Have you heard the theory of quantum memory?"

"No."

"It may only be my theory. At my age, it becomes hard

to distinguish one's own thoughts from other people's. But I believe it is scientifically proven that when atoms collide, which atoms do all the time, they leave an imprint on each other. Two shapes caused by the impact, which fit together— what a plumber would call male and female. And they're drawn back to that perfect fit. This, by the way, is possibly also the physics of love. And reincarnation."

She shifts position. For an active woman, being confined to bed is almost as bad as the illness.

"Do you see that painting over there?" Barbara points.

It's a long, narrow canvas, dark gray at the left side shading into a blaze of gold.

"I won't tell you who painted it, it's just distracting. He said it was a picture of my life. I kept it in a closet for a long time—it reminded me too much of what's gone. He moved on and painted other paintings, just as Micajah will write other songs. But you and I, we have to beware the danger of the muse. These beautiful things freeze us. They steal our life force. We have to reclaim our selves again."

"Did you love him?" Eve asks.

"Yes. I loved him. Thank you for asking. I did want to say that out loud. And that is all I want to say about it. You notice I am not asking you."

They share a smile.

"I loved again," Barbara continues. "And so will you. Don't hold it against Micajah. You and I were shaped by our parents, and they were shaped by their parents, all of us rolling along twenty-five years behind the times. But the times speeded up and the chain broke. That's why the young are so dangerous. The matrix of their world is entirely different. What shocks us is ordinary to them."

The next coughing fit saps her. The light dims in her eyes.

"I should go," Eve says.

Barbara's smile is wan and waxy. Eve wonders if, despite what Barbara said, she is dying and has known it for some time.

"The box is downstairs, in the kitchen," Barbara says.

"I saw it."

"Good luck, dear girl. Thank you for coming all this way. Will you turn off any lights, as you go?"

Eve would like to embrace her, as she did the last time she left this house. Feeling that it would be an intrusion, she doesn't. Nor does she dare to say goodbye.

For days, the box sits unopened in Eve's kitchen, just inside the door where she set it down when she carried it in from the garage. She's forced to step around it daily, yet she doesn't move it. There is no place in her house where it belongs. It cannot go into a closet—not yet, anyway. Besides, it may contain a bill, which she will have to pay.

She trips over it and panics that she may have damaged the precious object again—if Yann actually repaired it, which she doubts. The box will have to be opened. Just not today, she tells herself, day after day after day.

The box starts to take on a malevolent cast, lurking by the door. Maybe, she thinks, it carries a curse, as so many old things do. Deborah has always been suspicious of things that are *wabi sabi*, in the Japanese phrase—beautiful in their imperfection. Might it have survived Auschwitz, Eve wonders, and have been broken by its owner because he was forced to play it as his brothers trudged to their deaths? Might it have seen a pogrom or some other massacre, been gutted by shrapnel from bombers? Might it have crossed a desert on a handcart, the single useless item a refugee couldn't bear to leave behind, until one day, maddened by thirst, he shattered it with a stone?

Compared to such histories, Eve's pain is minuscule. Her heart is not broken. It was secondhand already and she buffed it up for Micajah, and then someone smudged it with dirty fingers. And, she, Eve, decided that she wanted to take it back. She could change that decision; she knows how to use a phone.

What she had was a fantasy. Of course it couldn't stand up to real life. Just like a delicious meal isn't meant to be eaten daily for breakfast, lunch, and dinner. Looking at it this way, Bethany is the equivalent of a clumsy waiter who spilled a drop of red wine on her skirt.

It's Sunday, and it's raining. Eve has no jobs to bid on or design. As she makes the first slice through the tape, she imagines Yann packing up the instrument, fetishizing the protective materials. Bubble wrap and Styrofoam peanuts seem too crude for his artisan's code. Probably he used sawdust, wadded newspaper.

She lifts the flaps. He did use styrofoam peanuts after all. There is an invoice—just for the cost of the peanuts. Across it is scrawled: "Breaks my fucking heart."

Even though she's prepared herself, she takes the disappointment hard. Yann was her only hope of getting the instrument repaired. The man in Paris might as well be on Mars. She's been counting on this chance find to solve her financial worries. But it seems she's reached a dead end.

She pulls the case from the box. Polish has been worked into its cracked leather. When she opens it, her heart leaps.

The instrument is even more beautiful than she remembers. Yann has waxed the wood to a deep sheen. She hadn't realized that some of the vines were broken off, but she sees he has restored the carving too, allowing the vines almost to run wild, but tempering their wildness with an artist's discretion.

She turns the instrument over, her heart pounding. The gash is gone. Yann has placed vines to mark where it used to be: seams whose meaning only he, Eve, and Micajah will ever know. As she follows the curving vines with her finger, she starts to cry. Only one other time in her life has she cried tears like these: when Allan was born and she saw that he was perfect.

The next day, Eve puts the whole big box, with all its layers of packing, on the back seat of her car and drives into the city. She cannot take the instrument on the train and the subway, or even in a taxi. It's the kind of thing that gets left in taxis. Irrationally, she fears that the force field of a taxi would wrest it from her. She goes early, before the parking garages fill up. She's lucky: she will only have to walk three blocks to the auction house.

This is what Yann meant in his note. But his prejudices are not her luxury.

She clasps the case close to her chest as she walks. It seems unreal: to be carrying something worth a hundred thousand dollars along a public street. I look like a crazy lady, she thinks, holding this so tightly; someone might think it's empty, or that I have my dead baby inside. If I was younger. Maybe they'd think I've been carrying it around for a decade.

She concentrates extra-hard on her footsteps, especially when stepping off and onto curbs. This is no time to trip and fall.

Inside the building, she makes her way to the back room, where the oak paneling and spotlights give way to linoleum and strip lighting. She takes a number from the ticket machine on the wall. She knows the drill from last time.

The well-brought-up girls wear cashmere twinsets now, as it's fall. They flit to and fro, matching up hopeful sellers with jaded experts. Eve asks for her expert by name.

"I'm not sure if he's in today," says the girl. "Did you make an appointment?"

Eve didn't think of that.

"I've shown this to him before," Eve says. "He thought it would be very valuable if I had it restored. And I have."

"I'll see if he's here," says the girl in a tone that suggests she's fairly certain he won't be, and disappears.

He is, though, and eager to see the instrument again. "Quite delectable," he says, stroking its repaired body as if it were the body of a lover, or—the thought appalls her, for what it tells her about her own mind—the body of a child he's about to eat.

"Six figures, as I said before," he continues. "And the first of them is unlikely to be vertical."

It takes Eve a moment to get his meaning. He's obviously pleased with his gnomic style of speech. Eve suspects he's been perfecting it over the years—probably because he's deeply frustrated. Either the instruments are uninteresting, and therefore bore him, or interesting, which means he wants them for himself but can't afford them. He's left with the thin satisfaction of disconcerting sellers with estimates much higher or lower than they expect.

His tongue flicks out to moisten his lips. His prominent Adam's apple bobs up and down.

"My secretary will help you with the paperwork. I recommend you choose to illustrate it in the catalogue. We must spend money to make money, as the sages say." As he settles the instrument back in its case, his fingers loiter on its curves. Dragging them away, he snaps the clasps shut, his long wrists and hands wrapping around the case like tentacles, pulling it toward him.

Eve reaches across the counter for the case. Surprised, he clutches on to it. It's nearly a struggle before he realizes he has to let go.

"I've changed my mind," Eve says. "Thank you for your time."

She walks rapidly down the short hallway into the display rooms, her eyes fixed on the exit, imagining armed guards chasing her down, preventing her escape with this treasure that she's stolen from those who should own it because they can pay. Her edginess subsides only once she's out in the autumn sunshine, heading back to her car.

She's known all along what must happen. Yann brought the instrument back to life not so that it can become a collector's trophy, but so that it can be played. Eve's role is that of father of the bride: to bestow the treasure on someone who will cherish it above everything.

If she keeps the instrument, she'll be holding it hostage against the day that Micajah might come back into her life. She could return it to Yann with a request to give it to Micajah, but that seems cowardly: a betrayal of love and nerve.

She drives toward Brooklyn.

She remembers telling the driver of the town car Micajah's

address, as he lay injured on her lap—injuries that he'd
brought on himself. She scrapes the ridges of her memory,
trying to recall it. No use: neither the street nor the number.

As she drives across the bridge, she recalls the ride on
the Vespa: the feel of the wind against her thighs, the moon
strobing along the cross streets, its shimmering reflection in
the East River. Did they turn left or right after the bridge?
All she remembers is riding down a long boulevard toward
the moon.

She finds a drugstore parking lot and brings up the subway
map on her phone. What station did she go to that morning,
her underwear wadded in her handbag? As she scans the map,
the station names start to come back: words she saw written
in tiles through her tear-blurred eyes. GPS will get her to the
neighborhood, at least. Once there, she can cruise the streets
until she finds the big metal door.

When she finds it, what then? Does she have to see Micajah
face to face? Her fight-or-flight reflex is screaming for flight.
But she can't just ring the bell, leave the box outside, and drive
off: what if he's not home? Could she leave it with a neighbor?
Does he have neighbors? Maybe she could find out the name
of his agent or manager, and send it care of them—but they
might discard it as some crazy fan gift and not even tell him.

There's the door, harsh and cold. She parks on the far side
of the street and sits in her car, looking at it. She checks the
windows up above: no sign of whether he's home. She hopes
he isn't. She does not want him to find her lurking there like

a stalker. And she is afraid that he will talk her back with the force of his green eyes.

But if he's not home, she'll just have to come back. She notices the address stenciled on the dark bricks, but that's no use. She can't send something so precious by UPS.

There is no way around it: she can wait like a cop on a stakeout until he comes outside or comes home—which could be hours, or weeks—or she can phone. It's been nearly two months, but she hasn't been able to bring herself to delete his number. A stronger woman would have.

Micajah answers after one ring.

"I'm downstairs," she says. "On your street. I have to give you something."

She hangs up before he can question her. As she waits, her imagination turns lurid: she could be waiting to give him a slap, or a gunshot.

There's a screech as the door slides back a few feet. Wary, Micajah stays in the open doorway. Eve stands next to her car, holding the instrument in its case. She sees shock flood his face as he realizes what she's giving him. Yet he stays where he is.

The last time she was on this street, her mind was as clouded and dim as the light. Eve still wants answers, but she doesn't want to confuse things. Now isn't the time to ask. Most likely, she will never know.

She crosses the street, puts the instrument in Micajah's hands, and turns back to her car.

"Eve. Stop. Please."

She keeps walking.

"I didn't know what happened till Bethany told me."

Eve clenches her ears, trying to deafen them. She hears him anyway.

"I didn't give her a key. She stole it. That day I couldn't pick up the Nova—"

Eve closes her car door against his words. She starts the engine.

In her peripheral vision she sees him move toward her. For a moment, she's afraid he'll do something drastic to hold her back. The instrument in his hand stymies him: he cannot drop it or throw it. He can only watch her drive away.

12

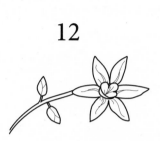

She's taken the pictures off the walls of the dining room and nailed up four large slabs of corkboard in a five-foot-thick stripe. She noticed those slabs of corkboard as she headed toward the checkout of the craft store, carrying modeling clay and some small tools. She can pin things up on them: pictures and quotes for inspiration, or plans, sketches, work in progress.

Funny, she thinks, I never did this for my garden designs. The sense of commitment feels good. It may not be specifically to the clay; she's not sure yet. But she's claimed the room, which was shared and formal, just as a homesteader would stake a claim, by pounding markers into the territory. In this space, she will make something out of nothing.

Eve has always tended to be responsible, cautious, even self-denying. She has always kept her home as if ready for inspection: everything tidy, with minimal signs of personal activity, particularly downstairs. Now she covers the dining table with plastic, taping it tight over the edges. She empties the decorative dishes out of the dresser and stashes them away; this will be her supply cupboard. The sparseness of the few packages of clay and tools on the shelves energizes Eve. They will not be sparse for long.

She hardly turns on the television or reads a book. Clay is all she wants. Some days she spends four, six hours at it. She sets herself tasks of increasing difficulty, like a pianist practicing scales: a beetle, a turtle, a bird, a cat. She buys an articulated wooden horse from a thrift store and tries to reproduce that delicate equilibrium between fineness and power. Most of her pieces, even the successful ones, she breaks down, melding them back into the clay's bulk. As she does so, she feels that she's infusing the clay with more potential. She does not yet know what she really wants to make. She does know that she will not arrive at it by rational means.

Becoming a good sculptor isn't the point. She's starting at a late age, and anyway she will never be Michelangelo or Rodin. The satisfaction comes with getting better, competence developing incrementally, a direct function of time invested. Still, she's not counting. When she is working with the clay, time disappears, and then progress comes in thrilling leaps that make her say out loud, just to hear the words, "I did it."

If she makes nothing of value, it won't matter. The claiming of space and time to do what she wants to do is victory.

A few times in the past she thought of buying some clay, but Larry's presence deterred her. She did not want to be watched, her output judged as if the results, rather than the doing, were what justified the time spent. Nor did she want to trivialize what she might do by treating it as a once-a-week evening-class hobby. Lurking in those thoughts was a sense that Larry exerted a degree of ownership over her time and energy, and that she accorded it to him as part of their marriage contract. Even after Larry began his spiritual practice, which by analogy allowed Eve her own solitary pursuit, she did not begin; it was tainted by the feeling of revenge, and tenuous if it depended for justification on Larry's agenda and on behavior that caused Eve pain.

So the urge lay fallow. Meanwhile, her business gave her the necessary excuse to take snatches of time for herself.

The pleasure of getting her hands dirty with the clay is like gardening, but without the hot sun, the labor of weeding, and the grind of profit and loss. Eve's mind wanders to the prehistoric cave paintings, the soot-stained fingers of the Cro-Magnon artists as they smudged aurochs and antelopes onto rough limestone with charred sticks. Everyone was dirty then, but—feeling a kinship across the millennia—Eve imagines that the artists held a special fondness for the resinous grime on their hands, the tracks of the animals they had conjured from nothing.

The more competent she gets, the prouder Eve is of the grit in her cuticles and under her nails that the nail brush can't reach. She feels like a revolutionary as she goes about her errands in the suburban archipelago of nail salons. She is quickly developing a hatred of them and their insistence that a perfect manicure is a requirement of civilization. Long nails are the modern equivalent of footbinding, she's decided: just another way to hobble women. To prevent them from actually doing anything for themselves under the guise of suggesting that they're so precious and desirable they don't have to. To induce learned helplessness.

Larry's Acura is still in the garage, a ghostly remnant of Eve's former life. She wonders if he will ever come and get it, or ask her to sell it for him. She'd like it gone. She'd rather feel like a woman with a future, when she comes home, than half of a defunct couple.

She takes a single grocery bag out of the back seat. It's light; she's pared her needs down to the minimum. It's November, she's got less than four thousand dollars in the bank, and she's looking at months of no work in the garden design business. She's hoping she can hold on financially until Allan returns from Cambodia, and he will help her figure it out.

Most days she tries not to think about it. She is too proud to tell her sisters, who are both on the other side of the country, wrangling teenagers. Bill's death created a distance between Eve and the two younger girls; they didn't feel the loss as deeply as she did, nor did they feel Eve's terror that Bill's wildness might be in them too. The three of them tried, over the years, to bridge the distance, but the bridges were weather-dependent: if life was easy, the bridges stayed strong, but in stormy times they weakened and sometimes collapsed, and when the sisters rebuilt them they were less robust. During those many years when Eve didn't want to admit how unhappy she was, they sagged away.

She takes off her coat, hangs it on the rack, then heads into the kitchen. The mayonnaise is on the counter, top off. Sitting at the table, eating a sandwich, is Larry.

"Hi, Eve," he says.

It's as if an eraser has wiped out her ability to speak.

"The job in Arizona wasn't the right fit for me," he says. "So I came home." His tone is light, as if this is good news and nothing particularly remarkable. But she detects anxiety behind the facade. This inner spark of knowing gives her something to hold on to.

"You don't live here anymore," she says. She hears her words as if they're being spoken by someone else.

"Of course I do," he says, adding with a sly grin, "wolves mate for life."

His attempt at charm turns Eve's stomach.

"You're a human," she says, "in a manner of speaking."

The managerial flatness of her voice, which sounds like a hospital receptionist, pleases her because it signifies not the dullness she used to live in, but an utter absence of feeling for Larry. She's looking at a familiar stranger: someone she knows well but doesn't care about at all.

Larry's eyes skitter sideways. "Blaine wasn't the man I thought he was. He didn't deserve my trust."

Eve stares at him.

"Sorry. If I hurt you." Then, realizing that's not enough, he adds, "I made a bad call."

And that, Eve knows, is all the apology she's going to get.

"Aren't you going to say anything?" He stands and approaches her. "Like, maybe, you're glad I'm back?"

She's too stunned to move away. He plants his lips on hers, hard, and for long enough that Eve wonders when he will pull away. Evidently, he feels it's more authoritative if it's a performance, even though the only audience is the cat.

She feels like a fire hydrant. That wasn't a kiss. It was a marking of territory.

She has to get away from him, figure out what to do. If she goes upstairs, he will follow her, and the likely result of that will be a pathetic attempt at sex. Her old self would have submitted; this self will not. She knows that Larry doesn't have it in him to force her.

She goes into the utility room under the guise of putting things away. On the floor next to the laundry basket is a pile of his clothes, left there for her to deal with, as she always did.

"You're not really an asshole," she says, coming back into the kitchen with an armful of his dirty clothes. "You're just acting like one because you don't know what else to do. I get that."

She dumps them on his lap. They bury the sandwich. Some fall on the floor.

"You don't live here," she says. "Leave. Now."

"It's my house too," he says.

"Fine. Then I'll go."

He reaches for her without getting up—this time, as if he's going to pull her onto his lap. Eve grabs the back of his chair and pushes hard. He tumbles backward, banging his head on the floor.

"What the hell, Eve. That's assault!"

She stands over him, wondering whether this is hate that she feels, or just contempt.

"You could have told me, Larry. That you lost your job. That you were planning to leave. You just pretended I didn't exist."

"It seemed easier," he says.

That word sends her over the edge. She kicks him, hard, in the ribs. He yelps.

"Liar." Her breath is coming in hot bursts. "You're a liar."

"Eve, I've never lied to you—"

"No, it was *easier* to say nothing! To let me think everything was okay. You were lying to yourself. Every pathetic little thought, trying to convince yourself you're right and noble and worthy of respect, every one of them was a lie. You lied to me for twenty-six years. You made yourself out to be an honorable man."

She kicks him again.

"Because it was *easier*! And I believed you."

She grabs the phone, dials 911.

"What's your emergency?"

Eve holds the phone away from her ear so that he can hear the voice and know she's not faking it.

"Police," she says. "An intruder in my house. But I think he's leaving. He'll find it *easier.*"

She's been transferred; there's no person there anymore, just ringing. Thank God it's not a real emergency. Who knew they took so long to answer?

"I took my suitcase upstairs," he says feebly.

"Let me," she says.

She goes upstairs, still holding the phone, and throws his suitcase out the window.

"My ex-husband," she says when someone finally answers. "He broke into my house."

She gives her name, address, Larry's name, the basic facts. She feels like she's in a movie, speaking dialogue that someone else wrote for her.

As she comes back downstairs, she sees Larry on the lawn, stuffing his dirty clothes into the suitcase through the half-opened zipper. She raises the kitchen window so he can hear her.

"He's leaving," she says into the phone, holding it away from her ear again so that Larry can hear the voice on the other end.

"You'll be hearing from my lawyer," he says, dragging his suitcase toward the garage. It's pitiful, this last attempt at dignity.

"Fine," she says.

The sound of his car recedes down the road. She pulls out the phone book and calls a locksmith.

How hard did she kick him? She has no memory of the resistance of his flesh against her shoe. She never imagined she could ever do something like that. This is domestic violence, it's not okay. It's no more acceptable for a woman to attack a man than for a man to attack a woman. She feels queasy.

This is where in the movie Eve would pour herself a drink, she thinks. Or punch the air. Or collapse in a torrent of sobs. Crying would be a relief, as if water might put out the flames of her fury. But no tears come.

She's disoriented. Her sense of time and space is fuzzy, yet the kitchen is crystalline in its immediacy: the ruddy beige of the granite countertop that she's always hated (that was the color on sale when they remodeled), the dent in a cabinet door where Allan slingshotted a penny at it, the tired magnets on the fridge. None of it has anything to do with her at all.

Not knowing what else to do, she sets the chair upright, throws away the sandwich, puts the lid on the mayo and replaces it in the fridge—then changes her mind and tosses the mayo, too. Larry was the one who used mayo. Why was it still in the fridge at all? Was it some subconscious wish that he'd come back? She should have thrown it out months ago.

When Eve wakes the next morning, there's a heaviness pinning her to the mattress. In the adrenaline rush of the previous day, she'd expected to awake feeling liberated, light, enthusiastic, energetic. Instead, it's like she's trapped under the rubble of an earthquake: shattered concrete certainties, sheared-off edges, the broken edifice of what she's spent her entire adult life building. The downward pressure of nostalgia—all the years she spent with Larry, the child they raised together, the home they created together—crushing her.

There are no rescuers. She will have to push her own way out from under the past. Every muscle movement feels like a step up the last ridge of Everest.

Eve had thought she was done with mourning. It's an ugly surprise that she is not. Here is another cache of dead dreams to mourn: the old hopes for what her life with Larry could be. Not that they were coming true, but now it's confirmed: they're aborted, miscarried. As wispy as the names she once thought she'd name daughters, other sons.

Before yesterday, she thought she'd take Larry back, if he came back. She'd gritted her teeth and tried to speed up the dreadful forgetting, categorizing Micajah as a dalliance, fleeting as a sunset. Her affair did not have to be a marriage-breaker, especially as the sequence of events was ambiguous. It was a ripple in the fabric of her life, not a tear. When she thought about Larry, which was more often than she used to—because that was the most effective way to head off thoughts of Micajah—she no longer felt angry or betrayed. She rolled out one possibility after another. What if she received a lawyer's letter asking for a divorce? Would she soak him for every cent or agree gracefully? What if she got a phone call to tell her he was dead? Would she cry or celebrate? What if he came back, begging forgiveness? For some reason, thoughts of kicking him out seemed unreal; literally kicking him hadn't even occurred to her. In one scenario, she behaved as if he'd merely been away on a business trip and she welcomed him home in their usual way: dinner on the table and whatever *CSI* he wanted to watch. (That was before she staked her claim to the dining room.) In another, he wept and pleaded and she, rising above her hurt feelings, offered forgiveness, though not without strings. The secretiveness would have to stop. He would have to respect her autonomy. But they could develop new mutual interests, travel the world together maybe, go away for weekends and try to fall in love again.

This was the main reason she thought she'd take Larry back: because she couldn't imagine being alone. She used to feel Larry's need for her like a dragging weight, but now, having cast it off for good, she feels light-headed, unanchored. She did not want to be single ever again: she would have dragged that weight of Larry to her grave.

Do I need someone to be of use to, in order to justify my existence? she wonders. Do I need someone to desire me, in order to feel alive? Do men ever think like this? She remembers her grandfather, after her grandmother's death: without someone to look after and protect, he got bitter and crotchety. Every man for himself, he'd say, screw the world—and now Eve can hear what he didn't say: *if there's nobody in it who has a use for me.*

13

It's been months since Eve has gone to yoga class, and when she and Deborah go for their regular post-yoga coffee, it's odd to see the same pictures of Hawaii on the walls, the for-sale shelf of hand-painted pottery, the cracked leather armchairs, the small rack of CDs by the cash register. Eve's life has split into before and after, and walking into before gives her a sense of vertigo.

As the barista makes their lattes, she sings along to the stereo.

"Lover we'll surrender to the sweet smell of nature . . ."

Eve feels the blood drain from her face.

"What's the matter, honey?" Deborah puts a hand on her arm.

Eve wants to lie, wants to say, "Nothing," but it's impossible. The song is dissolving all the neat stories she's been using to barricade Micajah into a corner of her mind.

"This song," she says and stops, hating the shake in her voice.

"Gorgeous," says Deborah. "Never heard it before. Should I have?"

"No."

"So? What's the big deal?"

"It was written for me."

Deborah stares at her with a this-does-not-compute look on her face. Eve glances at the barista, hoping she didn't hear. She could have shouted and the girl wouldn't have heard—she's paying them no more attention than she pays to the posts holding up the ceiling.

The song modifies into an instrumental section: the melody Micajah messaged her that night. The instruments sound exotic; it's bizarre and beautiful, with a hypnotic rhythm that's almost a lullaby. The kind of melody that sounds like something you've always known in the rushing of your blood, something that seduces you to want to hear it again and again.

The girl sets Eve's latte on the counter and moves on to the next order. Deborah is holding her coffee already, waiting for Eve to get hers. After a moment, Deborah picks it up and puts it in Eve's hand.

Still Eve doesn't turn away from the counter. "Excuse me," she says to the barista.

The girl looks up with the instant smile of the service profession. "Sure!" she says. "How can I help you?"

"This song," Eve says. "What is it?"

"Released today. Sick, right? We kind of can't stop playing it."

She points to the CDs on the counter.

"New band. This song isn't on it though. Direct download only."

"Thanks."

"No problem!" She returns to the machine, wiping Eve from her consciousness as if she'd never been in it. What if I told her, Eve thinks. She wouldn't believe me. She'd think I'm insane.

The coffee shop drops away: the chatter of conversation, the rasp of the espresso machine, the whoosh of cars driving by. Eve feels like she's standing in a column of warm moonlight: the song permeating her, alchemizing away the confusion and suspicion and pain that came in its wake.

Only when the song finishes and another one starts does Eve remember where she is. She turns to Deborah, but Deborah has already settled herself on a sofa in a far corner, absorbed in her phone. Eve's nerves start to jangle as the spell of the song wears off. She's regretting telling Deborah, but she'd have had to tell someone. This is too big to hide.

"So some guy wrote that for you," Deborah says with quiet seriousness as Eve sits down beside her.

Eve just nods.

"Like 'Angie.' 'Light My Fire.' 'Layla.'"

"I guess so."

"Wow."

Eve has never seen Deborah speechless before.

Deborah picks up the CD. Eve didn't notice her buying it.

On the back is the photo that was taken at the abandoned docks.

"Which one is he?"

Eve points to Micajah.

"Seriously?" That's Deborah's expression of disbelief.

The song on the sound system finishes. "Night Blooming Jasmine" starts again.

"The coffee girls sure love it," says Deborah. "Is that him singing?"

"No."

Deborah peers at the CD.

"He doesn't look *that* young."

"He's twenty-eight."

"So what's the problem?"

He's only four years older than my son. But that's not really the problem. "His world, I guess. It isn't mine."

"Well, duh. You could say the same about a hedge-fund manager. Or an astrophysicist."

"I don't think I'd fall for a hedge-fund manager or an astrophysicist. Anyway, I've never met one."

"You'd never met a hot young rock-and-roll musician before either. How'd that happen?"

"I knew his father in high school."

"And he was chasing you too?"

"Nobody was chasing me. It was an accidental meeting on the street, and we had lunch and . . . well, things happened."

"I guess they did."

Eve has never seen that look in Deborah's eyes before: as if her world has shifted on its axis. There's no hint of jealousy or judgment in her—just something closer to awe.

"Swear to me you won't tell anyone."

"If it was me, I'd be hiring skywriters! But don't worry, I won't say a word. Except one thing: why the fuck is that great song not on this album? Unless it's got some bizarro title."

"Probably the album was already finished when he wrote it. It wasn't that long ago."

Deborah is studying the photograph again. She's longing for the sexy details, Eve knows.

"Was he wonderful?"

"Yes."

Deborah smiles, acknowledging that Eve isn't going to tell any more.

"So why'd you break up?"

Eve has been dreading that question. A stock answer will just send Deborah into hunting mode—and worse, it will feel like a betrayal of what she and Micajah had. She twists her skirt in her hands, trying to find the right words.

Deborah pries Eve's hands loose and places them on her knees, her own hands covering them.

"It's okay, honey," she says. "Deborah's not as dumb as she makes out. I don't need to know."

Eve feels a rush of affection for Deborah. She's a monster, Eve thinks, but she's *my* monster. She wipes away a tear with her finger.

"I do own waterproof mascara," she says.

"Great," Deborah replies dryly. "You might want to use it."

So many questions.

Why the special release? Why not wait for the next album?

Why is Lowell singing her song?

Will anyone figure out that it's about her?

Will anyone—like journalists—want to find out?

First answer: because it's too good to hold on to. The band want to play it onstage, and if it gets bootlegged they'll lose out.

Or: because Micajah wanted to put it out there for me.

Or: because he put it out as a way of getting rid of it, getting it out of his personal life into the open air. It means nothing to him any longer; it's just a song for the band. Which answers the second question.

But Micajah's voice, off-key and gravelly, isn't good enough for a recording. He said that himself. Lowell's role in the band is to sing. That it's his voice on "Night Blooming Jasmine" explains nothing.

Eve isn't convinced that Deborah's oath of confidentiality will hold. Deborah won't deliberately break it, but she'll get excited and let it slip out. There's only one way to keep a secret, Eve's mother used to say: don't tell a soul.

Beyond her immediate circle, will anyone care? If she was

famous, or connected to someone famous, of course they would. It's impossible, she thinks, that anyone would believe a song so special could have been written about an ordinary woman like me. That's not a magazine story. They'd expect an artist, a kooky bohemian, a fire twirler living a nomad's life in an old school bus.

If anyone finds out that it's me and can't believe it, she decides, that's their problem. I can't be the only person in the world whose ordinariness is both real and a disguise.

The song is obviously a classic. Twenty, thirty, fifty years from now, people will play "beat the intro," sing along with it, fall in love to it. She clicks open iTunes and sees that it's the number eight download of the day.

She syncs her phone, then figures out how to buy a download of the song for Allan, wondering if he'll be able to get it in Cambodia. She emails him, telling him only that she loves the song and hopes he will too. He will write back to say yes, he thinks it's great too, and that they're playing it in Siem Reap, where the time is so far ahead that tomorrow is already nearly over, and then he will send Eve a YouTube link to some other song that is his favorite of the moment, though he doubts she'll like it. And he will be right.

Then she checks her inbox and sees an email from someone she's never heard of, with the subject line "Night Blooming Jasmine."

She's unsure whether she should open it. Why would anyone associate her with the song? Could a journalist have found her already—maybe the fat man who was at the photo shoot? If she opens the email, will that be some kind of admission? Maybe it's just spam—do spammers send out emails with subject lines taken from top ten hits, since nobody opens the I'm-in-trouble kind anymore?

She clicks. The email turns out to be from a law firm:

"Please forgive the informality of this communication," it begins. "Our client was unable to provide us with a physical mailing address.

"We act for Micajah Burnett. Mr. Burnett has requested us to convey 100% of the publishing rights in the song 'Night Blooming Jasmine,' words and music by Mr. Burnett, to you or any entity you name, in perpetuity. As the song has only been released onto the market today, monies have not yet accrued. We welcome your instructions as to how remittance should be made, and an address to which we may send the necessary documentation for your review."

Eve reads the paragraph again, and once more, before she's finally taken it in. She's not sure what publishing rights are, or how much money they might represent. Her mother always said that if something's too good to be true, that's probably exactly what it is. Still, it's hard not to hope. Despite herself, she looks back at iTunes. "Night Blooming Jasmine" is now at number seven.

Out hunting for things for Deborah's store, Eve wears shoes with a heel that put a sass in her walk. Not because she wants to be noticed, but because it keeps the fizz rising in her. She wants, urgently, to keep that sense of aliveness that the song has restored to her, after the months that almost smothered it and the decade or more in which she didn't even realize how dead she was.

In junk shops and at flea markets, Eve sees scrimshaw everywhere. Much of it is crude carving on whalebone. Maybe none of it was made for the purpose that Barbara suggested. Still, she thinks of those sea widows building their manless lives, closing their eyes at twinges of pleasure as they hung out the laundry or swept the floor or built up the fire.

Micajah, for her, has entered that whalers' realm. They parted; and now she has no idea where on the globe he is, chasing the leviathan of success. There are no reliable lines of communication, though here and there she might receive a message via a meandering route, conveyed by a chance encounter, which will tell her little and will be meaninglessly out of date by the time she receives it. That sight of him on television fits this category. She cannot know, at any given moment, whether he is alive or dead. She imagines that for those women, in a strange way, it stopped mattering. You could not get through years of separation and think in the physical dimension every day, of the dangers of place and circumstance; you would go mad.

As she sits down to her plastic-covered dining table and

pulls the damp cloth off the clay, she knows she should be working at her desk, on an unseasonal and lucky commission from a small township sixty miles to the west, but she cannot face it. She's playing hooky. The promise of those royalties allows her to.

She's not sure what she wants to make today: only that she wants to do what *she* wants to do, not another safe planting scheme. She loves gardening, but plodding on the treadmill, as she has to in order to monetize her one real skill, makes her feel dull-headed and lethargic—a feeling she is no longer resigned to. I'm getting bolshie, she thinks. About time.

At her work table, thinking of those municipal flowerbeds, she fashions a tulip. Poor tulips: once, more valuable than gold and treasured for their unique differences, now bred for uniformity, made to stand in regimented rows, the wallpaper of civic landscaping. She lavishes attention on this single one, pictures the tulip that would have sold for millions in seventeenth-century Holland, the tulip that would have been presented to Suleiman the Magnificent or the Emperor Akbar: something splendid. She makes it curvy and bulbous, with flaring petals that promise more, and gives it a long stem.

Holding it upright, she blushes suddenly at the idea that has sprung into her head. In the following weeks, she makes a peony, a jasmine flower, a raceme of lilac. Different shapes, which might provoke different sensations.

She locates a 3D printing service. Resin will be better than clay for her purpose. The printing isn't cheap; it cleans out her bank account to print three of the four. She does not know where next month's mortgage payment will come from. But she's come to think of these flowers as prototypes. If they do what she hopes they will do, she will get someone like Yann to create more beautiful versions for the finished product. And maybe recruit Deborah for the business and marketing side.

For now, she is still experimenting.

A FedEx envelope arrives, containing another large-format envelope on which is embossed—literally embossed—the five names of a Fifth Avenue law firm. This is not Larry's lawyer. In fact, he never got one. He sent her divorce paperwork downloaded from a legal website, filled out and signed, along with a deed giving her full ownership of the house. As the divorce is uncontested, it will be final soon.

The showiness of the envelope has Robert's touch. She wonders if Robert is actually with this law firm. His name is not one of the five, but it's possible they are all dead anyway. More likely he just chose it, spending his son's money before it's made. Micajah wouldn't argue: he'd let his father have his satisfaction. Eve cannot imagine him ever arguing about money. She imagines him working as Yann's apprentice, penniless, wearing his gold-leaf underwear and sleeping on the sagging sofa, utterly content.

As Eve reads the documents, her hands start to shake. This

annoys her. She does not want to feel powerless again. They are full of complicated legal jargon, which she forces herself to comprehend. She has to sign in eight places flagged with sticky arrows.

Between the last two pages, she finds a smaller envelope. Inside is a printout of an airplane reservation. On it, diagonally, is written: "Please use this. M."

The ticket is to Venice, in two months' time. The return date is open.

Eve has never been to Venice. She has an idea of it, of course: canals and gondolas and mysterious alleys and damp. She has some notion that the city is sinking—or perhaps it has been saved? There was a time it was all in the news, but she can't remember what happened, if anything.

As the days pass, Eve realizes that it's not clear from his note that Micajah will even be in Venice. Could he just be giving her this ticket as a gift? But why Venice, why that date, why not just a travel voucher to go wherever she wants to go?

She pulls her passport out of the filing cabinet where she keeps it along with other important documents. It's still valid. She will not have to commit herself to the trip by renewing it, or make the trip an impossibility by not renewing an expired one. She can torture herself with indecision for a while longer.

A decision would be just as bad, though. The choice not to go feels both brutal and cowardly. The choice to go feels like walking toward a spinning web of knives.

Perhaps Micajah will be in Venice if she wants him to be. Is she supposed to let him know? That feels wrong—like asking for him back, giving up the power she took when she cut off communication. If he wants to talk to me, she thinks, he has my number. And in that thought is an unspoken agreement with herself that now, if he does call, she will answer.

He doesn't.

A week before the date of the flight, another email arrives from the lawyer. This one informs her that his client has requested $10,000 to be wired to her bank account, as an advance against the royalties that will start coming to her in a few months' time.

14

Up until the morning of the day she left, Eve wasn't sure whether she would go. She made preparations she couldn't have made without that advance: buying a new suitcase (not wanting to use the one that matched Larry's); searching out flattering new dresses, comfortable boots, and a pashmina; getting a bikini wax and a pedicure. All but one of those things she could justify to herself as basic maintenance, which tight finances had forced her to let slide. And she'd need the suitcase eventually; she'd be going somewhere in the next year, even if it wasn't Venice.

She has lost ten pounds in the two months since the ticket arrived—the Larry weight, she called it to herself, which made it easier to lose. She'd have liked to lose fifteen.

In the Nordstrom's dressing room, trying on bras, she assessed herself dispassionately in the mirrors. When your finances sag, your breasts sag; even with hand-washing, her bras had lost their lift. The best of these new ones, in a different size, took another five pounds off her, at least. Her waist has returned. She still dislikes the lack of smoothness of her back around the bra straps, but there's no help for that, with the amount of weight the bra has to carry. This is where the shawl comes in.

I am not going to meet my lover, she told herself. Even if I go. We are not lovers anymore.

As the plane takes off, she wonders, is he on this plane? She is in Business Class. He is not. Could he be in First Class, a late boarder? She has visions of him coming through to find her once the plane reaches cruising altitude.

No. He wouldn't book her a worse seat than his own.

Could he be in Coach? That's possible. He might not have been able to afford two Business Class tickets. Eve knows that the fame comes much faster than the money.

When the seat-belt sign pings off, she is tempted to walk back through the main cabin to see if he's there. And if he is? She can hardly imagine a worse reunion, a pretzeled hug in the narrow aisle. And if he isn't, how silly she will feel to think he might have been.

She stretches out in her diagonal pod, chooses the alt rock station from the airline's audio programming, and opens her book. It's already dark outside, and there's a curtain she can draw around her for privacy. With luck she'll fall asleep soon.

She has never traveled alone. With Larry, she booked the flights and hotels, but she let him lead her from baggage claim to taxi rank, let him take charge of the daily demands of tourism, feeling protected by his presence in unfamiliar places. Not that she was less competent—in fact, she often had to tell him what to do—but she preferred that whatever it was, he be the one to do it. When, more recently, she has thought of traveling somewhere, she thought of going with a friend: Deborah, maybe. It didn't really occur to her, until she bought that suitcase, that traveling alone was possible.

After what she has done with Micajah already, getting on a plane to one of the most civilized cities in Europe with a return ticket in hand is hardly a risk. And the knives? She will guard against them by armoring herself with the present. No questions about Bethany; no thoughts of the future; nothing beyond the new bubble they will inhabit, light-filled and iridescent until it pops.

And if he's not at the airport? She will make her way into Venice, check into a hotel (she's searched online and reserved a room for one night just in case), book her return flight for a week later, and spend that time savoring art and history and treating herself like a rather thrifty queen.

"Sometimes you find love, and a storm comes through and destroys it, and you don't know if it will flower again." Micajah's voice.

Eve has been dozing. The voice is gone. "Night Blooming

Jasmine" is playing. Maybe it was her imagination, hearing those notes, that retrospectively created his voice.

Like shadows in her dream, she hears the steps of the flight attendants pass her cubicle. One set of footsteps stops exactly beside her, and Micajah slips through the curtain, perching on her seat like a child's painting of an angel, then fitting himself into the seat with her, lifting her dress, his finger stroking tiny ups and downs in time to the waltzing rhythm of the song he wrote for her, playing her like the virtuoso he is, drawing out her own internal music by instinct.

"Your *bistecca fiorentina*, Ms. Federman." The flight attendant's briskly cheery voice, just outside the curtain, startles her awake. She snatches her legs together—but they are already together, decorous under the blanket. All her clothes are in place.

As she eats, she pages through the in-flight magazine, and finds that Micajah did DJ a playlist for the airline. He booked me on this flight, Eve thinks. It cannot be a coincidence.

Leaving the plane, Eve walks slowly to Passport Control so that the Coach Class passengers can overtake her, looking for the square set of Micajah's shoulders, his loping walk. He's not among them. As she comes through the automatic doors from Baggage Claim, one of the last passengers, she scans the Arrivals hall. He is not there.

She feels her mood and her confidence deflate. Her spirit, disappointed, is as tired as her body. She will have to find her way to the hotel she's booked. She starts to rummage in her bag for the printout.

"*Scusi, signora.*"

She looks up into a dark face, worn by time and weather. The man holds out a sign reading SIGNORA EVE. Looking for her full name, she hadn't noticed the sign when she came through the doors.

She follows him to a taxi rank of boats. The cityscape is dotted with factories—not at all what she imagined.

They chug past half-submerged posts, which Eve soon realizes are road markings. Behind them, the industrial shoreline mists over, its smokestacks becoming optical illusions. Eve feels herself between worlds, guided only by the line of green-furred posts in the flat lagoon, being ferried by a taciturn boatman into the unknown.

Finally, in front of them, forms take shape in the haze: domes, narrow towers, growing in height as the boat draws nearer. The city is a mirage—heavy stone floating on water.

As impossible as we are, Eve thinks. Maybe this is the only place where we could see each other again.

When they enter the Grand Canal, the boatman cuts his motor down to its lowest speed, and Eve is struck by the quiet. The few motors she hears are specific and individual, coming and going. On either side, where the stone facades give way to open spaces, human voices color the air like birdsong.

The boatman pulls up to a dock on the right, leaps out, and secures a rope around a stanchion. He hands Eve's suitcase up to a uniformed bellman, helps her disembark, then departs. The motor's wake leaves a flourish in the water.

Eve follows her suitcase into a lobby more beautiful than any room she's ever seen: intricately painted walls, silver-speckled mirrors reflecting a dimly lit infinity of curlicued glass chandeliers, thick textiles of damask and velvet and silk. The bellman points Eve toward the reception desk. She's intimidated by the opulence of this room, the quiet authority of the staff. She feels a pang of panic. Why has Micajah sent her alone into this palace, which at this moment feels as sinister as something in a fairy tale? She cuts off this train of thought as a) ridiculous, b) irrelevant, and c) plain wrong. Micajah is not cruel. This is generosity: a Business Class plane ticket, and what may well be the most expensive hotel in Venice.

Probably, she decides, he is waiting for me. She looks once more, carefully, around the room, into the shadowy corners, the wing-backed armchairs that might hide a face. He's not here. Of course he isn't. If he was waiting for her, he'd have seen her and she would already be in his arms.

Would I? she thinks. She's still wavering about whether she wants it all to start again.

Standing there, irresolute, in this quietly purposeful room, she feels self-conscious. She moves to the reception desk.

"I didn't make the reservation myself," she begins. "I'm not sure what name it's under."

"You are the *signora* Eve?" says the man behind the desk.

"Yes," she replies with relief. "You were expecting me?"

"Of course." He slides a form across the desk and hands her a heavy gold pen. She fills out the form and returns it to him.

"This is my room? In my name?" She's not sure how to ask the question. She knows only that she doesn't want to be surprised when she enters it.

"*Certo.*"

"Alone?"

"*Certo.*" This time his tone has an edge to it, as if he is offended by the implication that the Gritti is the kind of establishment where guests are expected to share rooms.

"Is there a Mr. Burnett registered here?"

"I am sorry, *signora*, but we do not divulge the names of our guests."

How to put it? "Mr. Burnett made the reservation for me. I was under the impression that I was meeting him here."

She sees in the man's face a flash of compassion for the crushing awkwardness of the situation she's in. He is too professional to ask or judge, but he is human enough to relent.

"I am sorry, *signora*," he repeats, making a movement with his hands as if he is releasing a bird.

He gestures to the bellman to approach and hands him a key. "I wish you a delightful stay," he says with a little bow of his head, and turns his attention to a camouflaged computer screen.

The elevator, lined with tall mirrors of the same gray-mottled glass, feels to Eve like a dark version of Cinderella's coach. The prince is not waiting for me, she thinks. He is somewhere in the shadows.

Her room is small and precious as an empress's music box. She tips the bellman with a ten-dollar bill, too tired to deal with unfamiliar euro notes. As soon as the door closes behind him, she sinks onto the bed. Jet lag, the semi-sleepless night, the emotional roller coaster she rode downstairs, are making her light-headed.

She drags herself to her feet, and to the bathroom—a brightly lit time-jolt from the eighteenth century to the twenty-first. She brushes her teeth, then crawls between the crisp sheets and sleeps.

When she wakes, many hours later, she notices, on the writing table by the window, an envelope addressed simply "Eve." When she opens the flap, she sees that the inside is lined, luxuriously, with green-marbled paper. It holds a square card embossed with the Gritti crest.

"I'm glad you came. M."

Eve stares at the familiar slope of his handwriting sunk into the grainy weave of the paper, willing it to reveal more. Then she realizes there is something else in the envelope. She pulls it out: a page torn from a guidebook describing an abandoned monastery on the outlying island of Torcello.

Eve has dinner on the Grand Canal, on a floating terrace extending from the palazzo. Before tonight, she would have said it was sad to eat alone in a fancy restaurant. Yet the longer she sits there, with her black-squid-ink risotto (she deliberately chose the most exotic item on the menu), the better she likes being single at her table: free to spin tales about the people crossing the wide wooden Accademia Bridge, carrying satchels or leading small dogs on leashes, and about the other diners, mostly people of her own age or older, one table of men arguing heatedly in German, another family with a sullen teenage son and a preening daughter; free to tune them all out and immerse her senses in the gravity-defying city.

And to read more about the monastery on Torcello. In her room she googled it, and had some pages printed out by the concierge.

Nearly a thousand years ago, Torcello was more populous than Venice itself. When the lagoon silted up and the land got swampy, people moved away, to the growing city further away from the shore. Even the buildings were pulled down and carried away stone by stone. Some of the palazzos lining the Grand Canal were built with stones from Torcello.

Micajah has still not communicated with her directly. She's getting annoyed. Whenever a bellman or concierge comes outside, she thinks he might be bringing her a message, but no message comes. His silence makes her feel like she's being played.

An occasional motorboat leaves behind the sonic trace of its passing: the lapping of water against the wooden docks and the stone walls, the beat swelling and dying away, echoing in the disused water gates. A row of gondolas bobs in the water near her table, their low seats padded by gold-tasseled cushions. I could take a ride in one after dinner, Eve thinks. But alone? A gondola ride at night through Venice, one of the most famously romantic things in the world. It will be hard not to feel the absence of Micajah beside her.

She's reminded of the famous photo of Princess Diana at the Taj Mahal on Christmas Day or her birthday or her wedding anniversary, whatever it was—a day when Prince Charles should have been with her and wasn't—sitting on a bench, shoulders slumped, hands demurely on her knees, looking doleful and alone. After a first automatic rush of sympathy, Eve had wanted to slap her.

As she signs for the check, Eve thinks: I am enjoying this evening as much as any evening, ever. Early evenings with Larry were exciting, evenings with Micajah, delirious. But now, by herself, Eve understands how highly strung she was in those evenings. Wanting everything to be perfect, wanting the love to flow to her without the tiniest hitch, more aware of wanting the man to be happy than being happy herself. Wanting to say the right thing, wanting him to think her wonderful. Wanting to think him wonderful. Snatching at the moment before it vanished.

She decides that she will take a gondola. But first, she goes up to her room. The day before she left, a UPS package arrived: her prototypes, 3D-printed in a pliable composite material. She tucked the tulip in her suitcase. Now she slices open the bubble wrap with a nail scissors. There is her tulip, with the velvety soft surface of the real thing. She had this one printed in a creamy white, with a green stem.

It will make a good story that her flower had its first test-drive in a gondola.

She takes the stairs down, feeling the tulip move gently inside her body, the ridges of the petals stroking up and down. A tingle runs through her.

As she pays the boatman, she is positively glad to be single. She feels the boundaries of her self expand, filling the space around her, leaving no lack, no gap where a man should be.

The gondola tips and sways as she steps down into it, the wave splashing softly against the wood pilings of the dock. It takes an effort of concentration to move to the seat without falling, the tulip's petals pressing deep in the front of her abdomen as she bends over, touching a sensitive spot as she turns to sit down. She pauses, savoring the warmth. Perhaps that was one of the spots that Micajah found and tagged with a letter of his name. They are all hers now. She might share them again, with Micajah or with another man, but she doesn't yearn for it. This is a contentment she's never felt before. She recognizes it as happiness.

The boatman unmoors and pushes off, and begins to sing. Eve holds up her hand.

"*Per favore*, no."

He guides the gondola into a side canal, dark and quiet. The only sound is the drip of water sliding from the pole, the caress of the gondola's wake against the stone, the whispering echoes of far-off footsteps.

The velvet of the seat cushion is silky against the backs of her legs. There are other, loose cushions, dark blue with gold insignia. She plays with them: nestling them around her, propping up her legs to find the angle that makes the tulip most powerful. Tiny adjustments of position send pleasure coursing through her.

The rhythm of the gondola lulls her, a gentle push and then a glide, slowing, and another push, penetrating further into the dark reaches of the city. Dim reflected light shadows the pocked and crumbling plaster. The boat passes narrow alleys, closed off at the far end by blank walls. The air smells of lichen.

She clasps one cushion close, over her stomach. Tensing the muscles of her arms creates a corresponding tightening in the muscles of her core, which clasp the tulip tighter too.

She lets the smile steal across her face. In secret, the sensations branch and intensify. Eve clenches her toes, and warmth floods her legs. She leans her head back, and feels the air currents play across her throat. Her fingers knead the hard ridges of the embroidered gold crest. This is pleasure without a goal: as enveloping as a bath, uncomplicated by the twists of emotion. Only this object, the work of her hands, returning to her the energy she infused into it, multiplied a thousandfold.

She can move the tulip inside her without, to the eyes of others, moving a muscle. She can choose just how much to reveal or hide. Here in this gondola, on a dark night in a city where she knows no one, there is little necessity for concealment. What thrills her is the thought that she could go about her days like this, with a secret flower to sweeten them.

And if I could, she thinks, any woman could. There's no being good or bad at this: no skill, no learning curve. Only paying attention.

She imagines a coffee shop, a playground, a supermarket. Raw-skinned mothers, buffeted by their children's demands, closing their eyes for a quick moment's refuge. Old ladies feeling the life force again, reliving the past or imagining a future they'd thought was forbidden them. Women on the poverty line, aging fast with toil and worry, flooding with endorphins that make them feel beautiful. Women, like she used to be, who get through their days by averting their eyes from their desiccated dreams, finding a power of self-sufficient happiness they never knew they had.

15

Eve spends her days walking, getting as lost as she can in the back reaches of Venice where the tourists don't go. She wanders through churches and *scuole*, seduced by Bellini madonnas and the tender domesticity of Carpaccio. She imagines Casanova prowling, fixing on his next target, and courtesans teetering on ten-inch platform shoes to keep their feet above the floodwaters.

She visits the Peggy Guggenheim Collection, smiling to herself as she recalls that morning in Micajah's bed, her certainty now that the G-spot really is all in the mind. Their lovemaking seems long ago, a rogue event that inserted itself briefly between her old life and her new. She is getting used to Micajah's peculiarly distant presence, and rather likes it; his return into her life eases her, yet his absence absolves her of demands.

It's been four days, and she has heard nothing more from him. At first it seemed bizarre, but now she realizes it's entirely in character. By nature he's an ascetic, a hermit. He told her once that he hates crowds, hates the public gaze.

A reunion with her in Venice, at a luxury hotel, would feel false to him, even if it hadn't felt that way when he sent her the ticket. He's elusive even to himself: unsure of what he wants, allergic to expectations. He never pressed her, never made himself inescapable. Except for that one night—and look what happened.

She takes a vaporetto from the Fondamente Nove to Murano to see the glassworks. At the vaporetto station she notices the schedule for Line 12, which goes to Torcello. She does not read it. But that night, back in Venice, as she wanders through the quarter near the Arsenale after a plate of pasta at a cheap and cozy trattoria, she hears the notes she knows so well, edging up in half-steps: the intro to "Night Blooming Jasmine."

Could it be Micajah, calling her to him? It would be like him to put their meeting in the hands of fate: to park himself somewhere and play and wait to see if she passes by.

Her throat tightens. Her heart thuds, as if it's trying to drown out the sound. She wants to move toward it, wants to run in the other direction. The mixture of panic and yearning freezes her in place, as immobilized as Lot's wife.

Then she hears the drumbeat, the guitar, the band kicking in. It's just the recording, coming from a speaker. She sits down on the steps of a little bridge, waiting for calm to come, letting the adrenaline metabolize.

As she sits there, the music—his longing for her trans-muted into sound—imprints its waves one more time into the currents of her body. The familiar pattern is as powerfully intimate as his voice would be, or the touch of his fingers. This she will always have. But once she leaves Venice, she may never hear him, or feel him, or see him, again.

Only about twenty people live on Torcello now. Eve has to take a vaporetto to Burano, another island, with a wide street of ice-cream-colored houses and mountains of lace-edged linens for sale, and change there.

As the second vaporetto chugs north, the gleam of the sun behind a mist of low cloud gives the sky the dull sheen of much-handled metal. Eve is one of only three people headed to this far corner of the lagoon; it's still early season and the tourists haven't arrived en masse.

Micajah may not even be there. It's possible that he has directed her there to find something, something that he found for her. It might be a relief if he's not there. Though she has left behind the anger and the betrayal she felt that night in Brooklyn, she is afraid of falling back into the swamp of desire and being desired. She is a different woman from the one she was before she met Micajah, and the one she was before she left him, but her footing in this new independence still feels precarious.

Taking shape in the misty air is a church tower, then a church, then the island with its stone sea walls.

Grass sprouts between the blocks of the quay. The side near the waterline is mossy, with the mixed smell of growth and decay, thick and sweet and grassy, a smell that comes in gentle waves like the lapping of the water. The stones are pitted with age, as if the raindrops of centuries had left dents where they fell, but cut straight and square with civic pride, to raise the people above the marshes and mud. Eve senses the ghosts of those footsteps around her, so faint that in another century they will have faded away.

The walls that remain are low and crumbling, overgrown with flowering weeds and weedy flowers, straggling unpruned across the abandoned stonework. As she walks along a dirt path, Eve realizes there are paving stones beneath the drifts of soil that have covered them, turning civilization back into wild land again.

Eve feels, with sudden clarity, that she is in the center of her world, at the place where all the lines of her life meet. How can that be, she thinks, with Allan on the far side of the globe, in darkness while she stands in daylight?

Because he is living his life now, and I am living mine.

As she walks toward the church tower, heat rising from the old paving stones through her sandals, she sees Micajah sitting with his back against a crumbling wall. His black hair, his beautiful face, in shadow, his long legs angling into the sun. He holds the instrument she gave him vertically on his lap, playing soft, random notes.

When he looks up at the sound of her footsteps, she

recognizes something she'd never registered before: an alien, angelic transparency in his eyes.

Angels don't have human hearts. They don't know what it is to bleed. Eve remembers that Satan used to be an angel, the best and brightest of them all. She imagines the pitchfork in Micajah's hand, prodding her into sensation, tearing the veil of numbness away. She remembers him fucking her godlike on the edge of space with New York stretched out hundreds of feet below.

Ten feet away from him, she stops.

"I didn't want to find you here," she says.

"I'm an illusion," he says. "If that's what you want. Touch me and I'll vanish into thin air."

"Why didn't you tell me you'd be here?"

"Because then you wouldn't have come."

"And if you'd said you wouldn't be here?"

"You wouldn't have come either." His smile throws a cord over the space between them. "You like not knowing. Did you know that?"

"Yes."

Eve loved that sense of being seen that Micajah gave her. He came into her life like a new sun, and the true Eve flowered. She no longer needs his eyes in order to see herself.

"How long have you been here?"

"Four months. Reading in the archives."

"What about the band?"

"I quit. I owed it to them to stay until we hit. But all that wanting — you don't hear the noise of your own engine. Until you switch it off, and then it's peaceful. And all that time you had no idea how loud it was."

There is something monkish about Micajah, despite the very unmonkish experiences she had with him. She can imagine him in a scriptorium, preserving the knowledge of an unknown past and transmitting it into an unimaginable future.

"I don't know Italian," he continues, "so I had to use a dictionary. It was slow. But, finally, I found something about a jasmine viol. It was made for the mother of the Sultan of the Ottoman Empire."

"It's called a viol?"

"If it had strings and a bow, they called it a viol. They went apeshit with the shapes." He laughs.

"When was it made?"

"Late 1700s."

"Here?"

"Here. On Torcello." He gestures around to the absent walls.

"The monk who made it would have been as famous as Stradivari if he'd wanted to be. But I couldn't find his name."

He seems to admire this anonymity, even envy it. He embodies that same contradiction, of being both solidly grounded in the tasks of the day yet only delicately attached to the corporeal plane. When he played for her, she could see him leave his physical location in space and time. When he plays, she realizes now, he is at his devotions. It's not a performance. It shouldn't be public.

"But look what else I found." He gestures around at the small walled garden. The sun is just reaching a bank of flowering sage.

"Sage," says Eve. "Bees love it."

"The monks here made honey too," Micajah says. "But look. Look harder."

The garden is half cultivated, half wild. Weeds everywhere, but the flowerbeds are distinct.

"Syringa. Alyssum. Nicotina," says Eve. "Those are the ones I know. And jasmine."

Micajah says nothing, just waits. As she gazes at him, baffled, she feels a slight breeze blow her dress against her thigh, and the scent of alyssum drifts into her nostrils. Carried on the wind across the still water of the lagoon, she hears the chime of a church bell.

"It's a flower clock?" she asks, astonished.

"Do you think it could be?"

Eve looks around. "It's possible."

"*I fiori delle ore*," he says. 'The flowers of the hours.' Just that one line. I found it in the abbot's records. He doodled it in the margin."

She explores the garden, touching the petals and the leaves of the flowers. "They're mostly scented plants," she says. "For the blind, this would be a little paradise."

"Maybe he was blind, the monk who made this," Micajah

says. "I imagined him a mute, extra-sensitive to beauty. But maybe he was extra-sensitive to smell. Not the head gardener—just a lowly worker. He found Linnaeus's book in the library, or maybe he thought of the idea himself: instead of the grimly ticking clock, which was probably the only sound he heard all day, he could grow an organic clockwork powered by the sun and the rotation of the earth, that would parcel out the hours and instruct the monks when to sing the glories of God."

He's telling the story as if he's written it. Maybe he has, Eve thinks. His imagination is private. She senses that he shares it rarely.

"So he experiments, year after year, tracing the habits of the flowers he's chosen, learning their preferences for water, soil, and shelter, finding which ones grow well together, coaxing them into symbiotic patterns, striving to bring nature into synchronicity with terce, matins, vespers. He has to choose the hours of one specific day to focus on—so he chooses Midsummer Day. But year after year the clock seizes up and fails to strike a blossom on a crucial hour. This patient monk strokes the flowers to reassure them that they've done nothing wrong. They haven't disappointed him, they just acted as God directed. It was he who miscalculated, misplanted, miswatered, mismulched."

Eve laughs, liking the words.

"He sees in this unattainable beauty an image of the Garden of Eden." Micajah stops, as if waylaid by the thought.

"Go on," Eve says, "if the story isn't over."

"It's never over." He smiles at her. She knows he means their story, as well as the monk's.

"Next year he does better. He acquires an assistant, a young brother who has entered the monastery after an unhappy love affair with a married woman, and vowed never to think of women again. He solaces himself with the beauty of the flowers: he strokes their petals, he murmurs endearments to them as he once did to his beloved. They blossom for him. And when the old monk is no longer able to walk, one mid-summer dawn he's carried outside on a litter, propped against cushions, which are allowed him only because of his age and infirmity, to see the first flowers opening. When darkness falls and the jasmine blooms, he takes his last breath."

"They would have buried him in this garden," Eve says. "They would have consecrated some earth for his grave."

"Gardening is like music," Micajah says. "The temporary conquest of entropy."

Entropy: the tendency of things to fall into chaos. Order is fleeting, and precious. Eve's mother was wrong: something too good to be true *can* be true—but it can't last long.

"We should play for them," Micajah says.

"The flowers?"

"Come here."

Tentatively, she approaches him, still nervous of being drawn back into his force field. Love for him is nearly over-whelming her.

"Sit," he says, settling himself against the stone wall and beckoning her to sit in front of him, his legs on either side of her. Above him, the branches of an apple tree bend into an arch, dotted with tiny fruit.

She leans back into him—their first touch, sightless, after so many months apart.

He rests the viol on her knee.

"You play it," he says.

A shaft of pure terror runs through her. What if the sound she makes is an ugly screech, an insult to this beautiful thing and to everything it stands for? The viol feels strange as she tries to fit her body around it: how to shape her hands, her arms, her legs. When, finally, she's ready, Micajah places his left hand over hers, gentling her fingers onto the viol's neck. With his middle finger he presses on hers, holding a string taut.

With his right hand, he brings the bow around in front of her, inviting her to take it. She does, and he places the fingers of his hand over hers in a half-embrace.

She notices that she's stopped breathing.

Micajah moves her hand closer in, making the bow hover just over the strings. Rotating his wrist—and hers—he adjusts the angle. She wills herself to loosen her wrist and abandon herself to his guidance, knowing that any tension in her body will mar the sound.

He clasps her infinitesimally tighter. She feels the barest touch of the bow against the lowest string. The pressure increases, firm and steady. Then he draws their joined hands to the right.

A long note, deep as a well, takes form in the still air. We made that, Eve thinks. Micajah and I, together.

He guides her hand back, close to the bridge again. The fourth finger of his left hand presses her fourth finger down onto the second string. Again, his right arm embraces her a fraction closer as he brings the bow onto the viol. Again, he draws their joined hands to the right, a longer note this time, a little higher.

The sound waves linger in the air. Eve imagines the flowers drinking them in, transforming them into greater depths of color and scent.

For a third time, Micajah moves the bow back to the strings. His left index finger guides hers onto the third string. But just as she expects him to bring the sound into being, he lets go, his hands poised above hers. This time, she forms the sound herself. The note falls somewhere between the first two, bringing them to completion.

"You could restore this garden," Micajah says. "I rented a house here. You could stay."

It would be an idyll: a summer snatched out of time, the hours marked by the blossoming of flowers. Then Eve thinks of her other flowers, and feels a burst of excitement about what she, herself, is in the process of creating.

She moves away and turns to face him, brave enough now to meet those gold-flecked green eyes.

"My flight leaves tomorrow," she says.

"You could change it."

He stands, his hands shaping themselves to the concave curves of her waist. She remembers how perfectly fitted they felt there. Beneath her hands, his waist feels lithe and strong, like the trunk of a tree that bends with the wind—a birch, or an aspen. She used to imagine holding onto him in a storm.

"No," she says. "I can't."

She does not want to withdraw from the world. She wants to dive into it in a way she never has before.

"The vaporetto will be back soon," she says. "I need to catch it."

As they walk back to the dock, they hold hands lightly. They have not kissed yet. Eve imagines how it will happen, in this warm golden sunshine: the rippling water, the scatter of orange poppies and wild thyme growing in the chinks between the paving stones, the chug of the vaporetto's engine hurrying their goodbye.

They reach the dock as the boat comes in. Leaning against a wall not far away is a backpack. Micajah drops her hand to go and retrieve it.

"You're leaving Torcello?" Eve asks, confused.

"I decided I'd wait a week for you," he says. "I rented the house in case you'd want it."

"So you weren't going to stay with me, if I stayed," she says.

"No."

They board the vaporetto and stand by the rear railing, alone.

"Last night in my dream, you kissed me," he says. "We were saying goodbye."

"Where are you going?" she asks.

"Istanbul. Then on from there."

She looks back at Torcello, its dome and towers dissipating into the haze. The viol has taken this trip before: from Torcello east to Istanbul.

"It's a quest," he says. "Like mining—going deep into the mineshafts of music. I want to find what's there. Kurdistan. Yemen. Iran. Afghanistan, if I can get in. Central Asia. The Pakistani borderlands."

He's dark enough to pass for local in many of those places. Eve imagines him in the winding lanes of souks, in bandit-pocked mountains, carrying this valuable thing. Drawing complex, twisting melodies from it. Maybe giving up his life for it.

"It's all about the search," he continues. "You don't decide what you're looking for. You let the treasure find you."

I wasn't looking for the viol that day it called to me, Eve thinks. Or for you.

He pulls a ring of keys out of a pocket of his backpack and gives them to Eve.

"Here, in case you need a place in Brooklyn. I changed the lock."

She smiles back at him, grateful. It might be good to start a new life there. She doesn't need an explanation about Bethany; they're beyond that. And whatever it was that battered him in the past—the story that Barbara spoke of—seems tangential now. He has never brought it up; either he doesn't want to tell her or it's tangential to him too, and in either case she has no need to ask. As she sat by Barbara's bed, she saw it as the key to a door that, by then, she no longer wanted to open. She had thought knowing about his past would lead to understanding him. That it would "explain" him. Now it feels like a simplification, as if he were no more than the product of a recipe, which could be reverse-engineered if she knew some of the ingredients.

She walks with him over little curved bridges, along quiet alleys, until they emerge onto the piazza facing the Grand Canal. On their right, wide steps lead up to the train station. The canal here is busy with the everyday labor of Venice: the loading of merchandise on and off boats.

"I'm going east," Micajah says, setting his backpack and the viol case on the marble paving. "And you're going west."

He puts his hands on either side of her face. Her hands settle in the small of his back, her fingers tracing the map of his spine. Their kiss is more tender than passionate, like white flower petals edged in red. Their lips linger, unwilling to break away.

Eve is the first to pull back—ravenous, suddenly, for the green depths of his eyes, the flecks of gold.

"I do love you," she says. She remembers his word, pure:

love without expectations or explanations, relying neither on the past nor the future.

"I love you, Eve."

He picks up his backpack and the case. Before he turns away, he strokes her underneath the eye, as if he's wiping away a tear that she hasn't yet cried.

"The world is round," he says. "Maybe we'll find each other on the other side."

Acknowledgments

My gratitude to:

Gabriel Morgan, for his intelligence, imagination, humor, and faith. Without him, *Say My Name* would not have come into being.

Joan Juliet Buck, for her indomitable belief in me and this book.

James Navé, for inspiration and teaching that made me a writer, and a keen editorial eye.

Rosie Johnston, Tara Lupo, and Andrew Harvey, for valuable criticisms and insights. Also, Tish Vallés, Lara Santoro, Helena Kallianiotes, Ruth Gavin, Lisa Wright, Cheryl Nichols, Christine DeHerrera, Anjelica Huston, Anais Rumfelt and Jason Cooper.

Sarah Gillespie, for the song "Night-Blooming Jasmine," specially written for this book.

Sonali Wijeyaratne, for two decades of encouragement.

Roger Landes, for introducing me to the music and the instruments that Micajah plays.

Bob Heflin, EMT, for advice on the collision between the town car and the Vespa.

Hank Spangler, for research that resulted in the wipe-my-butt highway.

Sally Williamson at HQ, for her incisive editorial suggestions, and Lisa Milton, for her gleefully enthusiastic support.

Margaret Marbury and Kathy Sagan at Mira, for their belief in this book.

Caroline Wood, my superlative agent.

The French translation of "Jabberwocky" is by Frank L. Warrin, Jr., and first appeared in the *New Yorker* in 1931. It came to me via my father John Julius Norwich's commonplace collections, *Christmas Crackers*.

Topics for Discussion

1. Micajah is a catalyst for Eve's new adventures and, in the end, her independence. Do you think her transformation would have occurred if she had never met Micajah? How does Micajah's interest in things beyond the mainstream inspire Eve?

2. Eve's marriage has been less than rewarding for some time. Would you say that Larry has faced this truth before she does? Do you think Eve would have stayed in the marriage if Larry hadn't left? Would you call Eve's journey a midlife crisis? Are midlife crises inevitable? Might they be valuable?

3. Music is an integral part of the story. Do you see any parallels between Eve and the musical instrument she buys and has restored? Why does Micajah feel he would lose his soul if he continued on the rock star path?

4. Gardening and flowers are recurring images throughout the book. What do they represent, for you?

5. Barbara is the kind of woman Eve would like to be twenty-five years in the future. Does anyone in your life inspire you in a similar way?

6. Bethany's attitudes to sex, intimacy, and relationships differ from Eve's. Are these differences purely generational? Do you believe that Bethany uses the generation gap as a weapon? How do you think Bethany would behave if Eve were twenty-five?

7. A woman's pleasure for pleasure's sake has long been considered taboo in many cultures. And often, sex toys are designed as substitutes for a man. Would you describe Eve's Flowers as sex toys? Should all pleasure lead to orgasm? Do you think Eve will be successful in commercially producing these products? Would you try one?

8. Do you think Eve and Micajah will meet again? Is there more for them to explore together?

9. Ultimately, *Say My Name* is a story about a woman finding independence and fulfillment alone. Do you agree with the author that this is a happy ending? Would this kind of ending have made sense to readers thirty, fifty, seventy years ago? Do you think the choice to be single is a happy ending particularly for women in midlife, or particularly in the times we live in? Do you think Eve will remain single always?

ONE PLACE. MANY STORIES

Bold, innovative and
empowering publishing.

FOLLOW US ON:

@HQStories